SPIDER-MAN loves mary Jane

The Unexpected Thing

collection editor JENNIFER GRÜNWALD
assistant editor CAITLIN O'CONNELL
associate managing editor KATERI WOODY
editor, special projects MARK D. BEAZLEY
vp production & special projects JEFF YOUNGQUIST
research JESS HAROLD
svp print, sales & marketing DAVID GABRIEL
director, licensed publishing SVEN LARSEN
editor in chief C.B. CEBULSKI
chief creative officer JOE QUESADA
president DAN BUCKLEY
executive producer ALAN FINE

SPIDER-MAN loves MARY JANE

The Unexpected Thing

WRITER
Sean McKeever

SPIDER-MAN LOVES MARY JANE #4-5 & #8-13
ARTISTS
Takeshi Miyazawa
with Rick Mays (#13 Flashbacks)

SPIDER-MAN LOVES MARY JANE #6-7
ARTISTS
Valentine De Landro
with Takeshi Miyazawa (Framing Sequences)

COLORIST
Christina Strain

LETTERER
Dave Sharpe

COVER ART
Takeshi Miyazawa, Norman Lee & Christina Strain

ASSISTANT EDITOR
Nathan Cosby

EDITORS
MacKenzie Cadenhead & Mark Paniccia

SPIDER-MAN CREATED BY STAN LEE & STEVE DITKO

SPIDER-MAN LOVES MARY JANE: THE UNEXPECTED THING. Contains material originally published in magazine form as SPIDER-MAN LOVES MARY JANE #4-13. First printing 2019. ISBN 978-1-302-91978-8. Published by MARVEL WORLDWIDE, INC., a subsidiary of MARVEL ENTERTAINMENT, LLC. OFFICE OF PUBLICATION: 135 West 50th Street, New York, NY 10020. © 2019 MARVEL No similarity between any of the names, characters, persons, and/or institutions in this magazine with those of any living or dead person or institution is intended, and any such similarity which may exist is purely coincidental. **Printed in Canada.** DAN BUCKLEY, President, Marvel Entertainment; JOHN NEE, Publisher; JOE QUESADA, Chief Creative Officer; TOM BREVOORT, SVP of Publishing; DAVID BOGART, Associate Publisher & SVP of Talent Affairs; DAVID GABRIEL, SVP of Sales & Marketing, Publishing; JEFF YOUNGQUIST, VP of Production & Special Projects; DAN CARR, Executive Director of Publishing Technology; ALEX MORALES, Director of Publishing Operations; DAN EDINGTON, Managing Editor; SUSAN CRESPI, Production Manager; STAN LEE, Chairman Emeritus. For information regarding advertising in Marvel Comics or on Marvel.com, please contact Vit DeBellis, Custom Solutions & Integrated Advertising Manager, at vdebellis@marvel.com. For Marvel subscription inquiries, please call 888-511-5480. Manufactured between 8/16/2019 and 9/17/2019 by SOLISCO PRINTERS, SCOTT, QC, CANADA.
10 9 8 7 6 5 4 3 2 1

Spider-Man Loves Mary Jane #4

Monday...

Well, look at *that.*

And I wanted to know if-- Harry, are you listening?

Uh-huh...

Your hair's disintegrating.

Uh-huh...

Wow. I haven't seen her look like that since *Homecoming.*

Yeah, the first *hour* of it, maybe.

Shush.

Holy *hotness.*

I tell ya, she really *does* it for me.

Yeah, whatever. She's nothin' special.

What's with *her?*

No clue...but she's *definitely* gotta be taken *down* a notch. Or fifty.

Hey. *You* sure look happy.

Yeah?

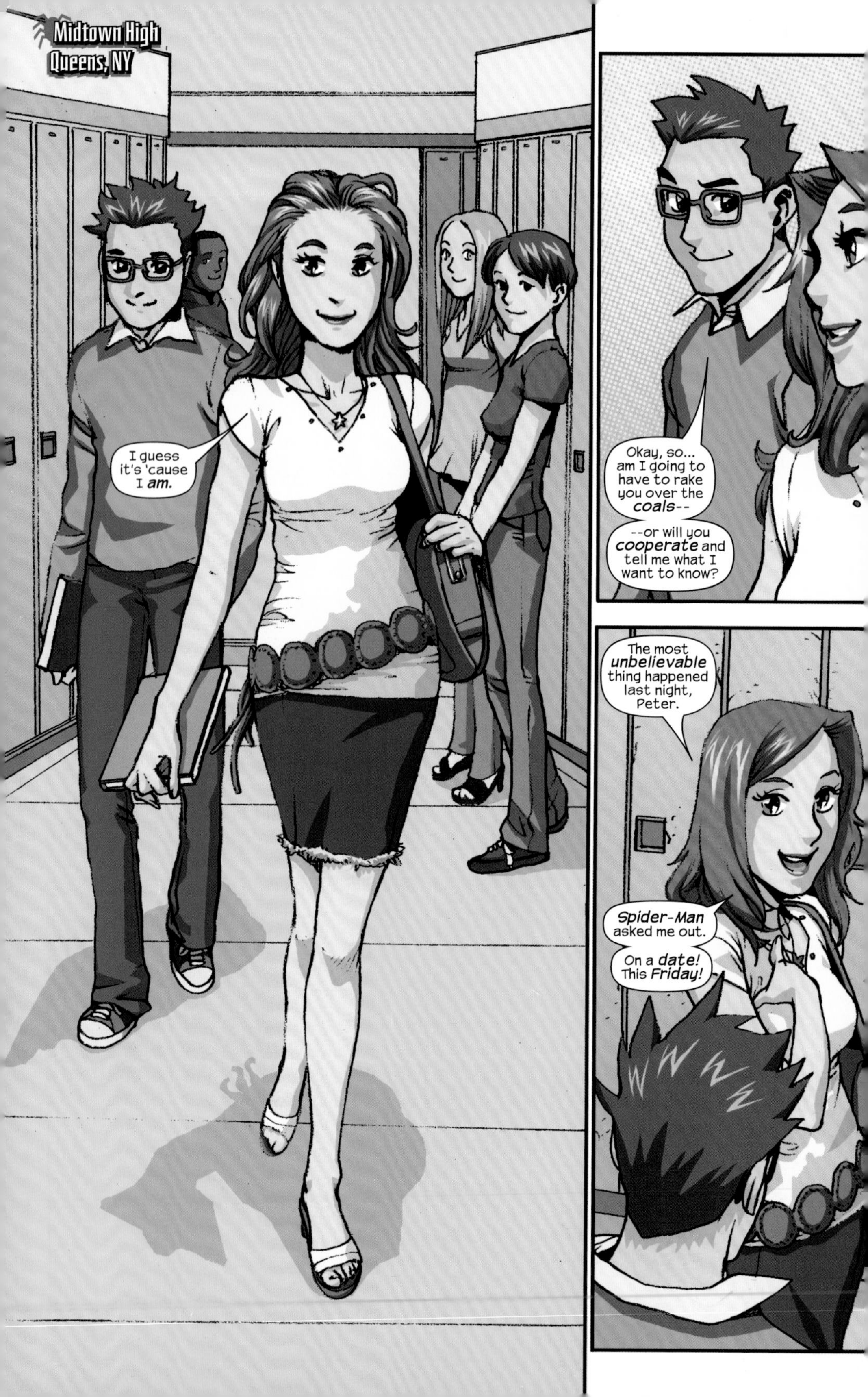
Midtown High
Queens, NY
I guess it's 'cause I *am.*
Okay, so... am I going to have to rake you over the *coals*--
--or will you *cooperate* and tell me what I want to know?
The most *unbelievable* thing happened last night, Peter.
Spider-Man asked me out.
On a *date!* This *Friday!*

No kidding! Well, that's--

Wow, I guess you're finally getting what you've been *looking* for, huh?

That's fantastic.

It's great to see you *smiling* like that again.

Like what?

Like nothing could ever bring you down.

Um...

Anyway.

I gotta get to class, okay? See ya!

HA!

Take *that*, Mary Jane Watson!

So... what's your *secret*?

What? I don't have a secret.

Oh. So you actually *are* deliriously happy for no apparent reason. No, that makes perfect sense.

It's *not* a secret, Liz. Not from you, it's not.

Reeeally.

So, you gonna tell me?

Sure. Right after--

NEW CHALLENGERS, PEOPLE!

Gonna tell me *later*?

Meet at the *Bean*?

You're *on*, missy. I can't *wait* to hear this.

You're being serious.

Seriously. No joke.

Ohmygosh, MJ!

I know.

Ohmy*gosh*! It's, like, so unbelievable I can't *believe* it! So, when's this *happening*?

Friday.

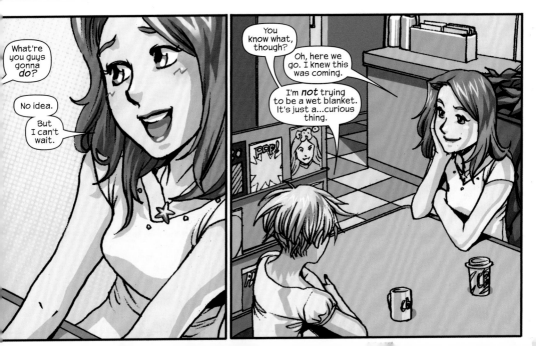

What're you guys gonna *do*?

No idea.

But I can't wait.

You know what, though?

Oh, here we go. I knew this was coming.

I'm *not* trying to be a wet blanket. It's just a...curious thing.

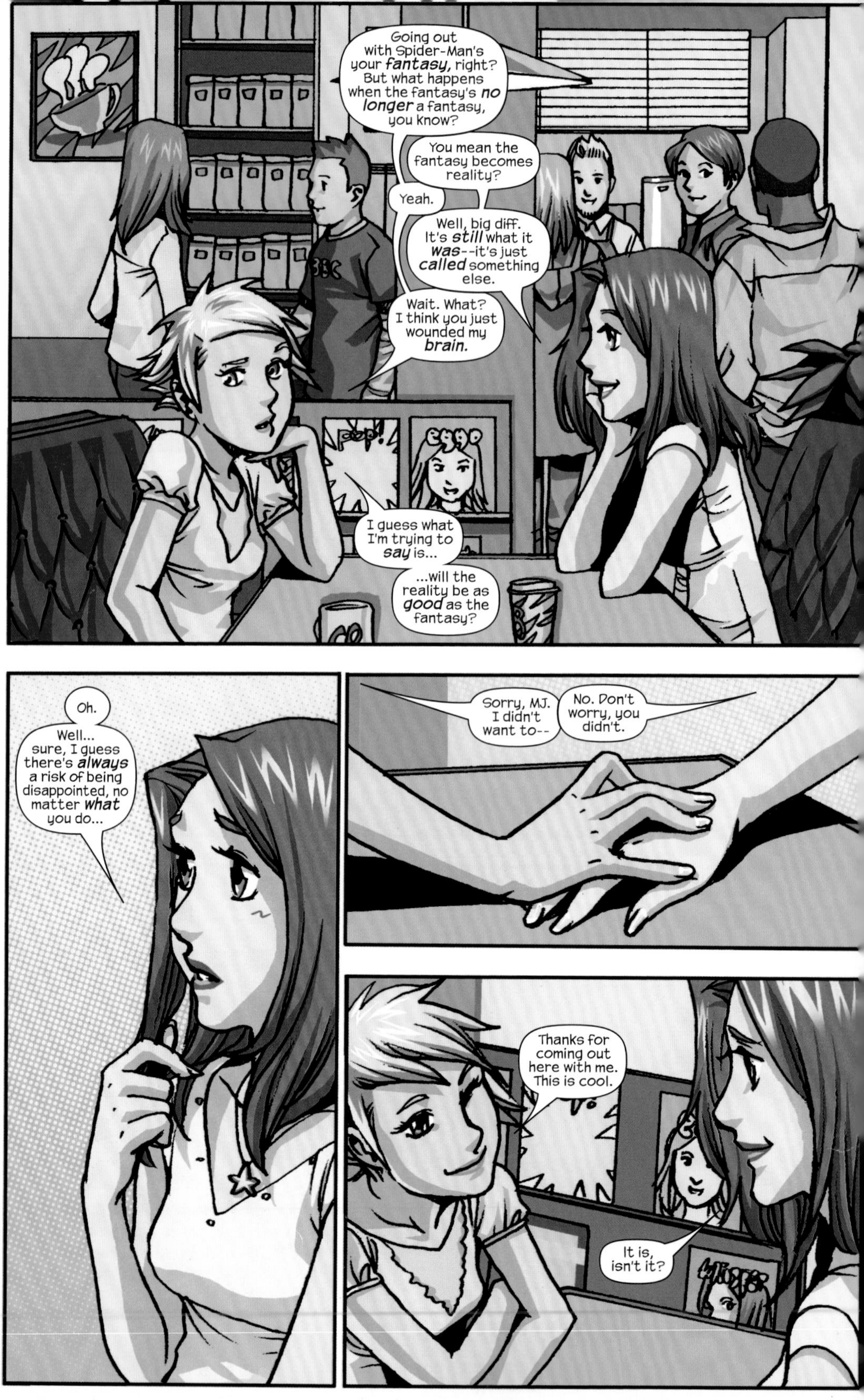
Going out with Spider-Man's your fantasy, right? But what happens when the fantasy's no longer a fantasy, you know?
You mean the fantasy becomes reality?
Yeah.
Well, big diff. It's still what it was--it's just called something else.
Wait. What? I think you just wounded my brain.
I guess what I'm trying to say is...
...will the reality be as good as the fantasy?
Oh.
Well... sure, I guess there's always a risk of being disappointed, no matter what you do...
Sorry, MJ. I didn't want to--
No. Don't worry, you didn't.
Thanks for coming out here with me. This is cool.
It is, isn't it?

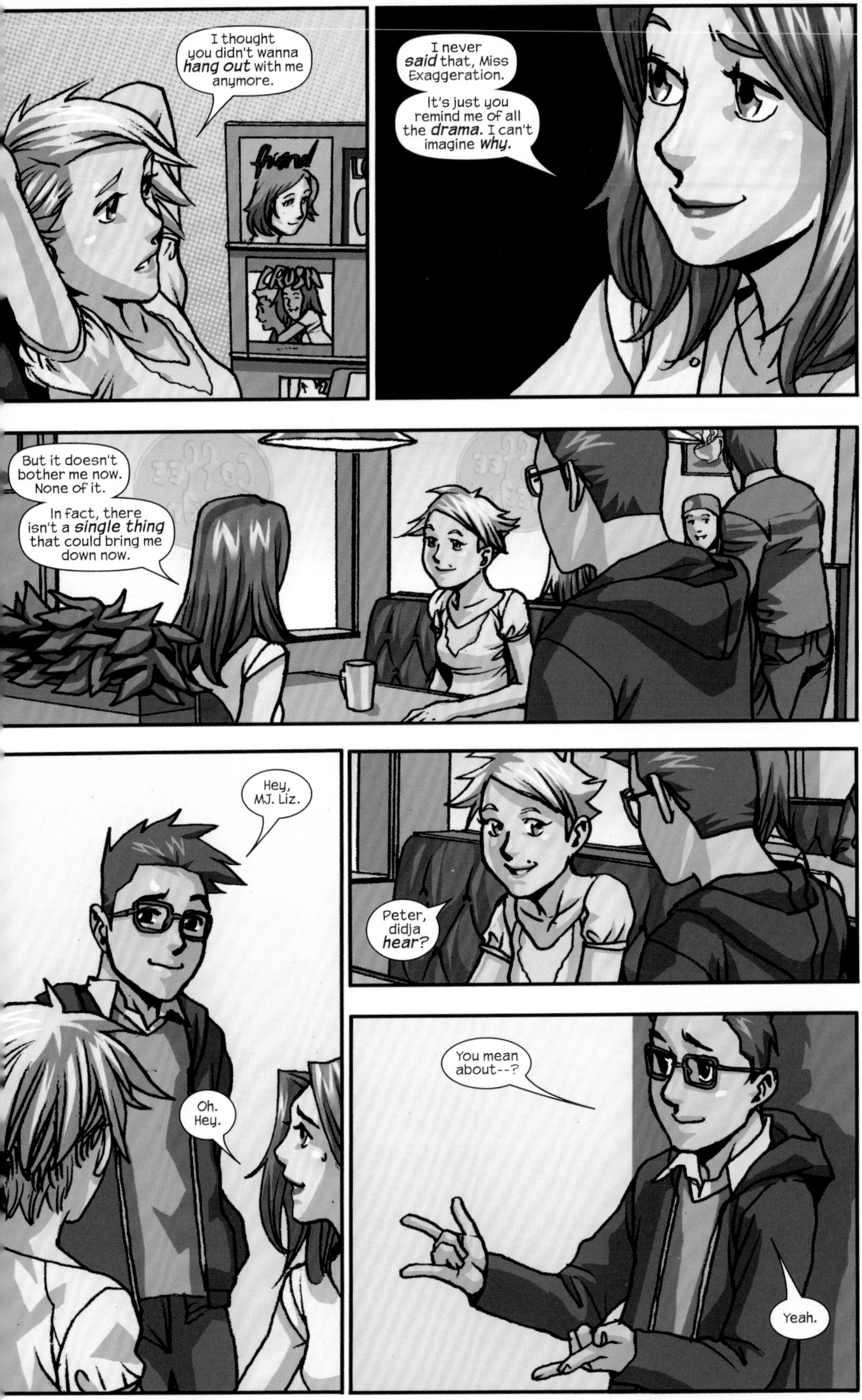
I thought you didn't wanna **hang out** with me anymore.
friend
CRUSH
I never **said** that, Miss Exaggeration.
It's just you remind me of all the **drama**. I can't imagine **why**.
But it doesn't bother me now. None of it.
In fact, there isn't a **single thing** that could bring me down now.
Hey, MJ. Liz.
Oh. Hey.
Peter, didja **hear?**
You mean about--?
Yeah.

Hey, uh...I got your message from my aunt. She said you can't *study* tonight?

That's right. I've got a thing. For the play?

Oh. Well, that makes sense. Just wanted to make sure, is all.

Um.

MJ, I was kinda hoping that we could--

Could what?

Peter?

Igottago.

Well, *that* was hardly awkward *at all*...

Whatever.

You *know*...

...dweebs like Parker don't do a thing for *me*, but still...he seems to be a pretty *stand-up guy*, don't you think?

He's really... real. Like an *actual* person.

We're just *friends*, Liz.

What? I didn't *say* anything...!

But I *do* think he really cares about you, MJ.

Tuesday...

Mary Jane.

Mary Jane!

You *moved* to your *right*.

Yeah? Isn't that what I'm supposed to do?

Sweetie, you're supposed to move *stage* right?

You went *stage left*.

Tch.
I should *know* that by now. I'm such a dork. Heh...

Krista, this is driving me *crazy!* She was *miserable* last week...! It's like she's *untouchable* now!

I dunno what to *tell* you, Lindsay...

Maybe there's a special *guy* in her life?

Boy, that *play* is really gobbling up your *free time* all of a sudden.

But you're having *fun,* right? More fun than *learning algebra,* at least.

Sorry, Peter. I've been *meaning* to--

Oh, hey, I wasn't insinuating--

I mean, here we are, on our way to a *meteorite exhibit.* If you didn't wanna spend *time* with me...

Still excited about the *big date?*

'Cause, you know, if you *want,* there's a documentary on *Bose-Einstein condensates* opening Friday...

Yeah, that sounds *really* tempting. Not.

Hey, come on. You can swing around the city with some dude concealing his hideously scarred face *any* old time--

--but how often do you get to share a tub of *unsalted, unbuttered popcorn* with a guy who can recite the *periodic table* in reverse without pausing? Hmm?

Peter...

Think about it: you don't even *know* this guy!

But me, I babble on so much that you know practically *everything* about--

Peter.

I am *NOT in the MOOD.*

HEY! STOP!

GIVE IT BACK!

Did you **see** that? What **was** that?

Oh, man. You know, I just realized... I can't go. I can't.

Peter, **don't**.

I promised Aunt May. I promised I'd help her.

I can't--

You can get home okay, right?

Thursday...

He *ran off?*

I felt really bad. I didn't mean to *hurt* him like that.

I mean, I *did* mean to, I think, just not *consciously*. He's just gotta *understand*, Liz!

I can't go down that *road* with him if I'm gonna start dating *you-know-who*...

So...it was *tough love.*

Right. Exactly.

Well...maybe that's not the kind of love he *needs* from you.

Not funny.

Good. I wasn't *trying* to be. I mean...

...do you *wanna* go down that road with Peter?

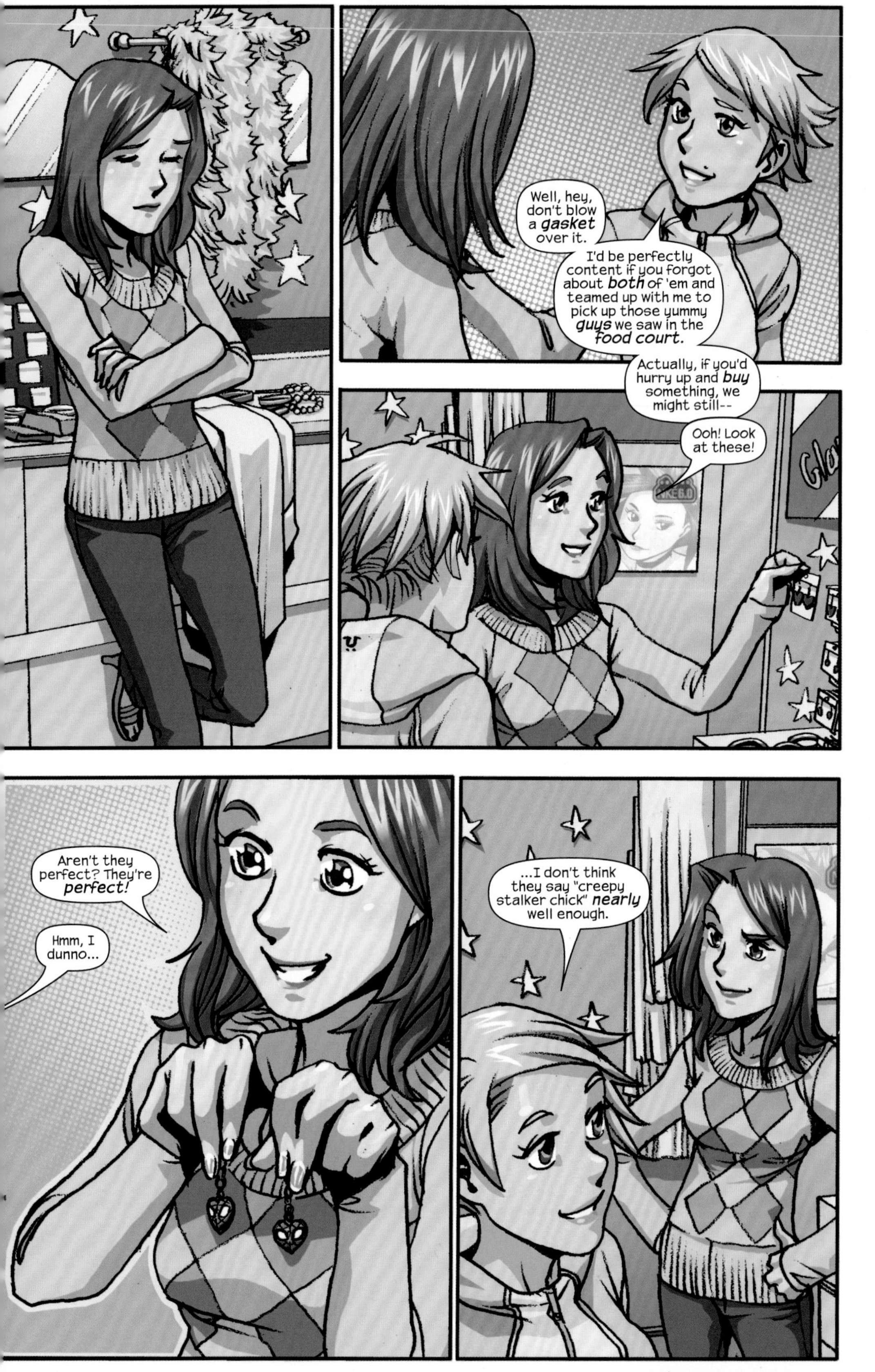
Well, hey, don't blow a *gasket* over it.
I'd be perfectly content if you forgot about *both* of 'em and teamed up with me to pick up those yummy *guys* we saw in the *food court.*
Actually, if you'd hurry up and *buy* something, we might still--
Ooh! Look at these!
Aren't they perfect? They're *perfect!*
Hmm, I dunno...
...I don't think they say "creepy stalker chick" *nearly* well enough.

Have you thought about what you guys're gonna actually **do** tomorrow?

Well, he **said** it's a surprise, but **whatever** we do, I'm sure it'll be--

HEY!

Thanks, ladies!

HEY!

WHOA!

AAAA!

I believe these are yours?

Hey.

Hey yourself.

So... uh...

If you hurt her in *any way*, I'm gonna *kick* your costumed *butt!*

Liz! Get a *hold* of yourself!

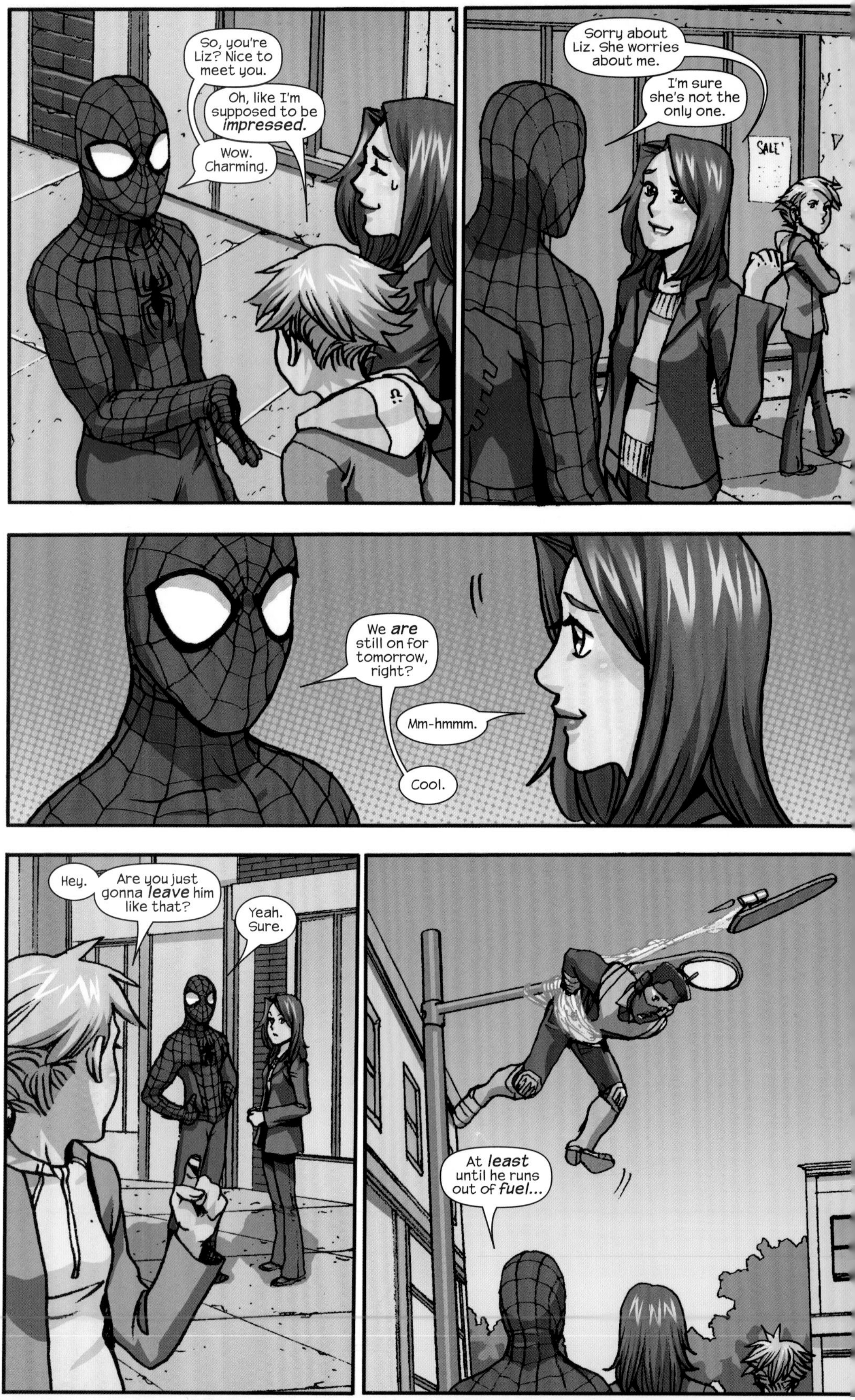
So, you're Liz? Nice to meet you.
Oh, like I'm supposed to be *impressed.*
Wow. Charming.
Sorry about Liz. She worries about me.
I'm sure she's not the only one.
SALE
We *are* still on for tomorrow, right?
Mm-hmmm.
Cool.
Hey.
Are you just gonna *leave* him like that?
Yeah. Sure.
At *least* until he runs out of *fuel...*

Friday...

Let's see...

Money... calling card... breath mints...

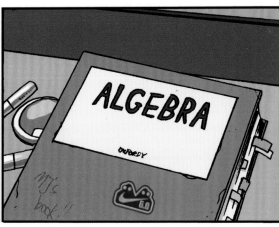

ALGEBRA

So silly...

Ohmygosh. I can't believe this is really happening...!

Spidey, you just hit the--

}HHH!{

Peter?

Are you here for *algebra?* It's Friday, you know.

I have that date? In fact, I was just about to...

Uh...

Don't go out with him.

Go out with me.

Peter.

You're always such a *kidder,* Pete. That's what I like about ya.

I gotta go meet Spidey!

Wish me luck!

The Fantasy Thing

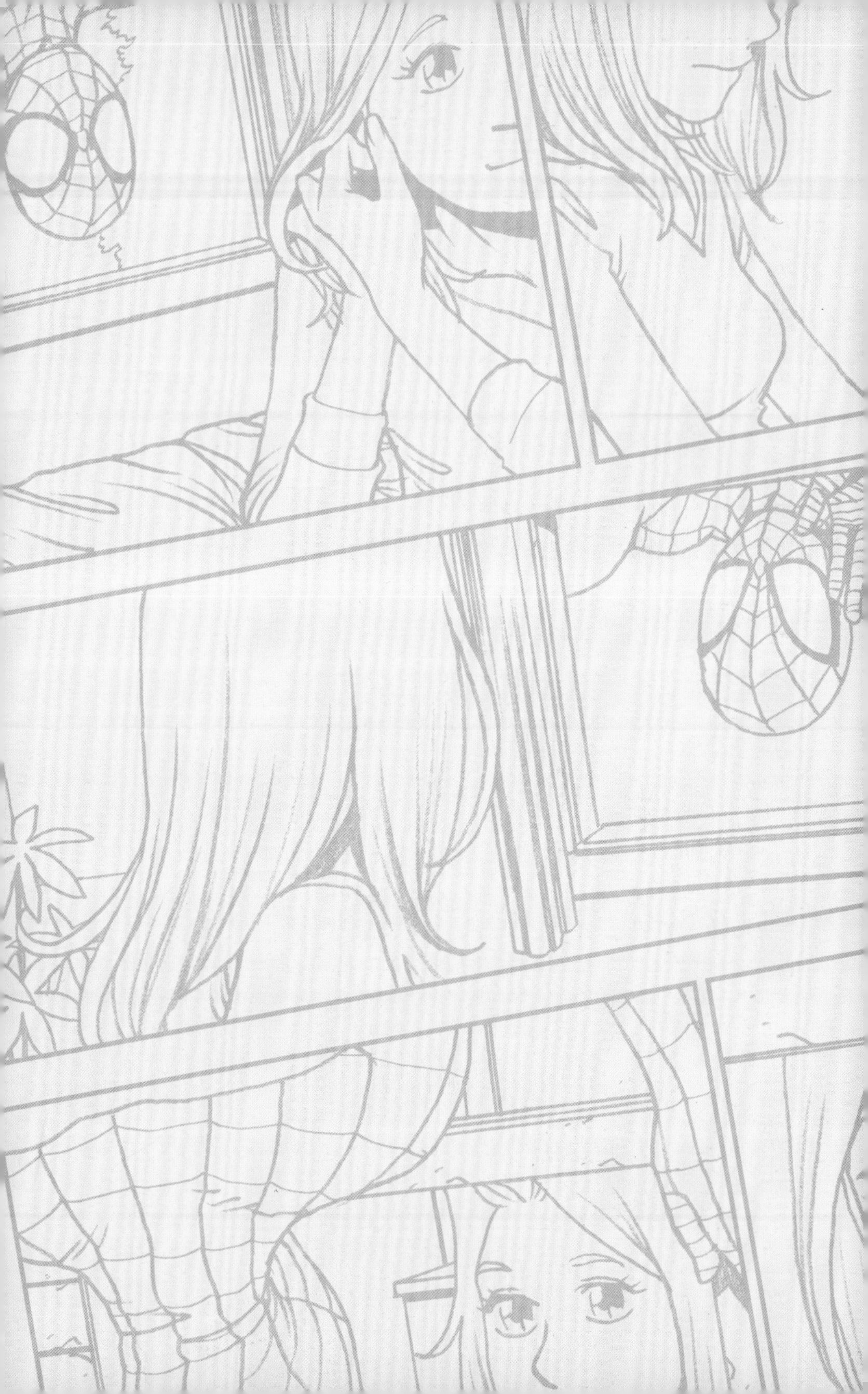

Spider-Man Loves Mary Jane #5

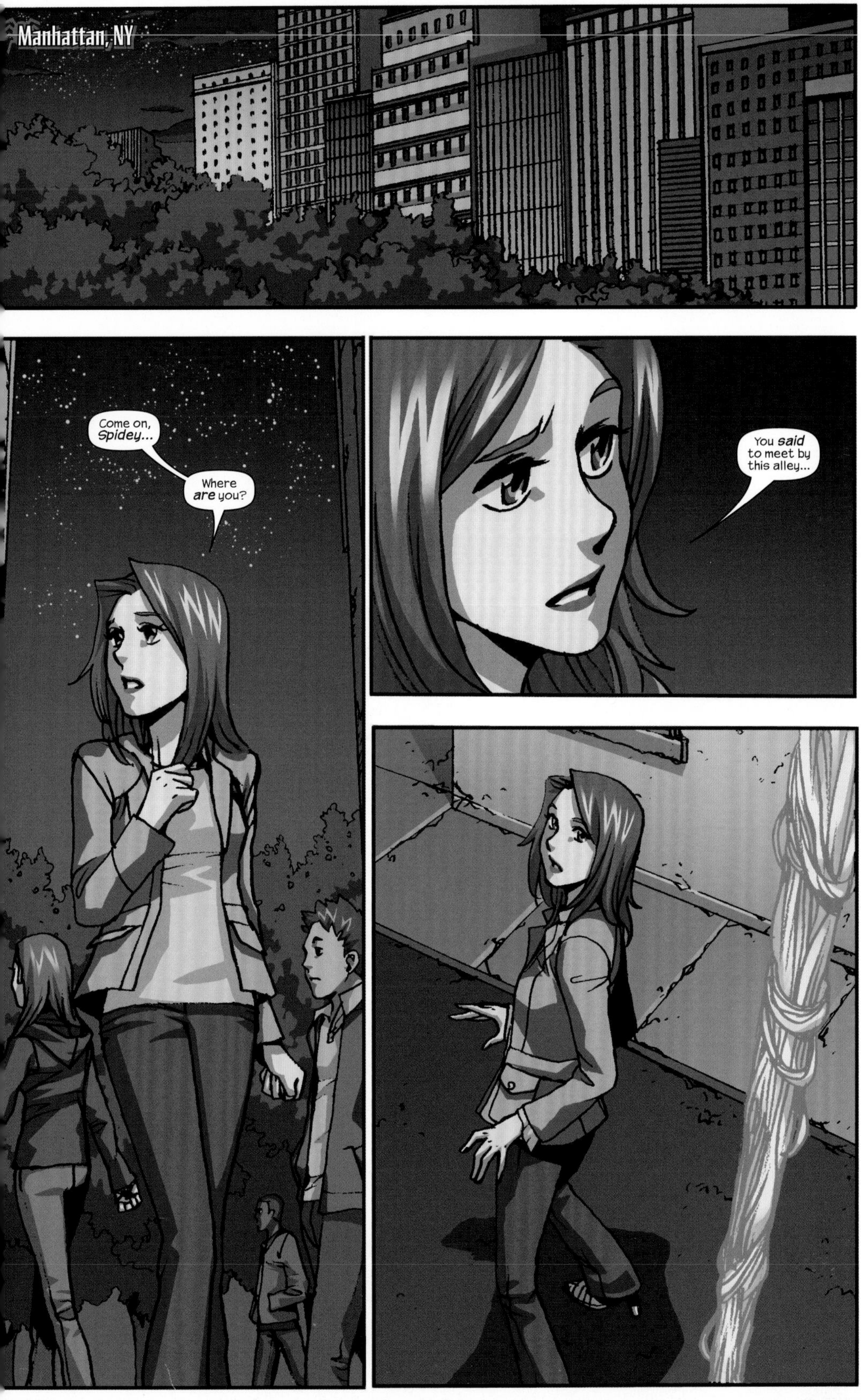
Manhattan, NY
Come on, Spidey...
Where are you?
You said to meet by this alley...

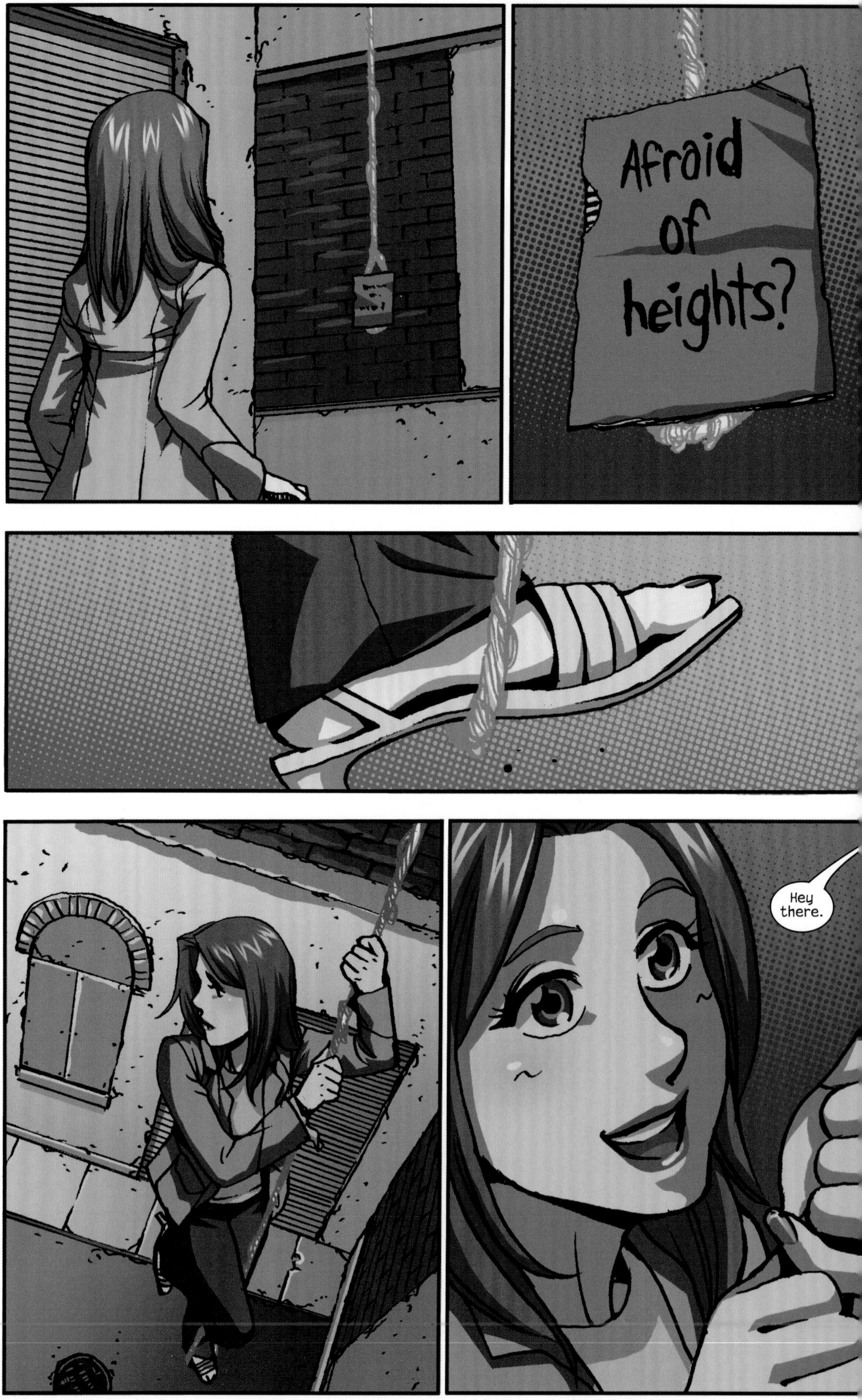
Afraid of heights?
Hey there.

Ohmygosh. You made a *picnic!*

I did, yeah.

And as you can tell, I *spared no expense* on the contents...

We've got peanut butter and jelly. We've got red delicious apples. We've got water. And, for dessert--

WATER

--macadamia-nut cookies.

This is--

This is really--

But why here? Why in this alley?

Because...

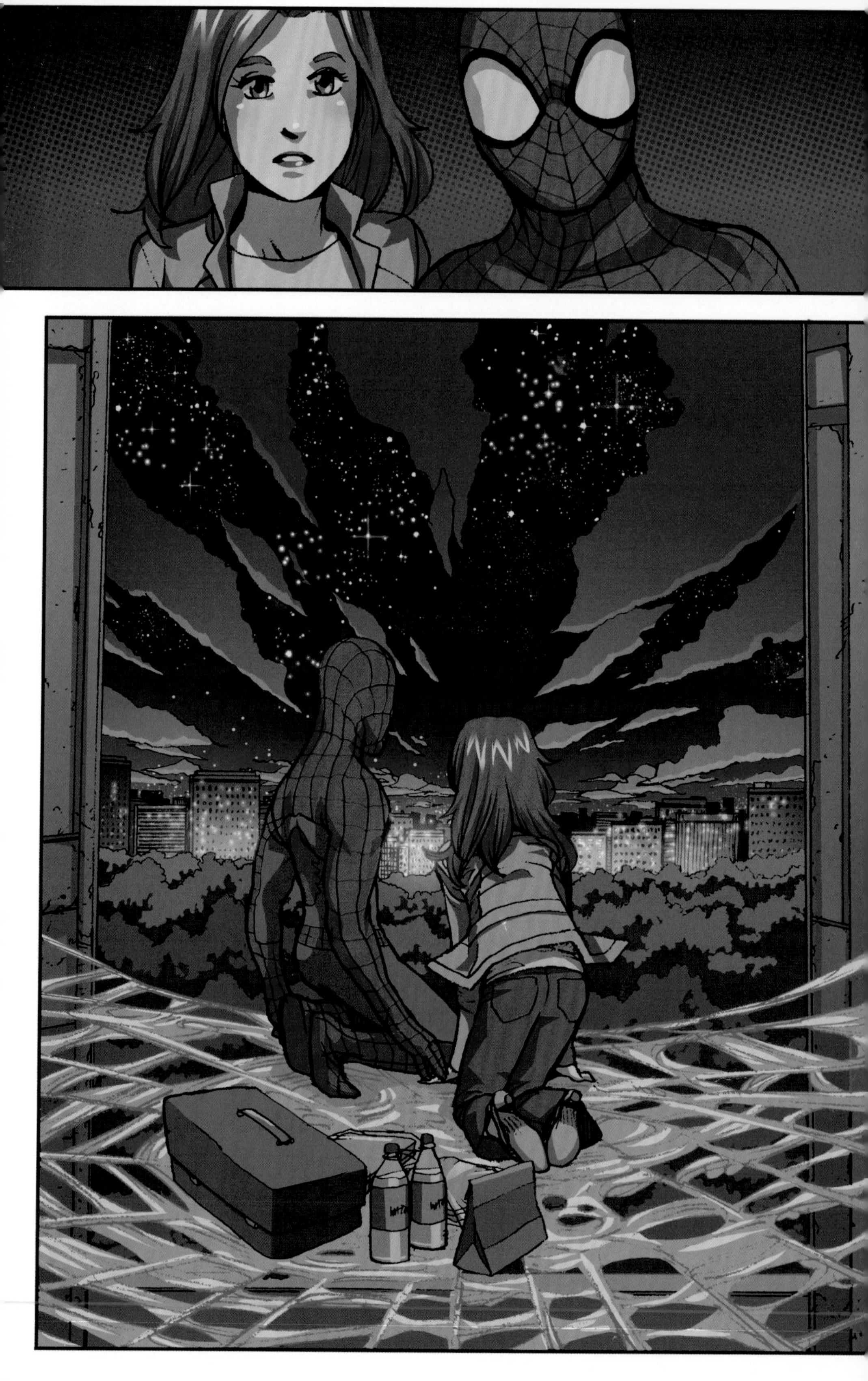

Thanks. This is really great...

...but it would make me feel a lot better if you'd pull up your mask and join me.

Oh, I don't, uh...I don't eat.

Not people food, anyway...

Heh! I'm *joking!* Honestly, I'm normal. Mostly.

I think.

So...when you're not, you know, wearing *that* or doing *super-hero* stuff--

CHOCO

en

COOKIES

Ah. Could, uh... could you not *ask* me about... that stuff?

Oh. Okay, sure. Uh...

Okay, well...

I saw the other day that you stopped some guy named *Hypno Hustler* at a rave?

I mean, I *know* you all have weird names, but what's the *deal* with--

Um...

NO!

Won't let you--

That purse would *never* go with your wardrobe, pal!

Uh--

Uh--

Heads up, miss!

Sorry 'bout that.

No. No, it's...

Why do you *do* it?

I mean...you can do whatever you want. Why are you so... unselfish?

Oh, I'm *plenty* selfish, believe me. I get a lot of *satisfaction* out of helping people.

Yeah, but you could just, like, *take* stuff and no one could stop you.

I guess *Mr.* and *Mrs. Spider-Man* raised a *good* boy.

Do your parents *know* that you-- Oh.

Sorry. Forgot.

What? What is it?

I wonder if it's *too soon.*

Hmm, maybe it *is* too soon...

Too soon for *what?*

Think it's too soon after a meal to go for a little *spin?*

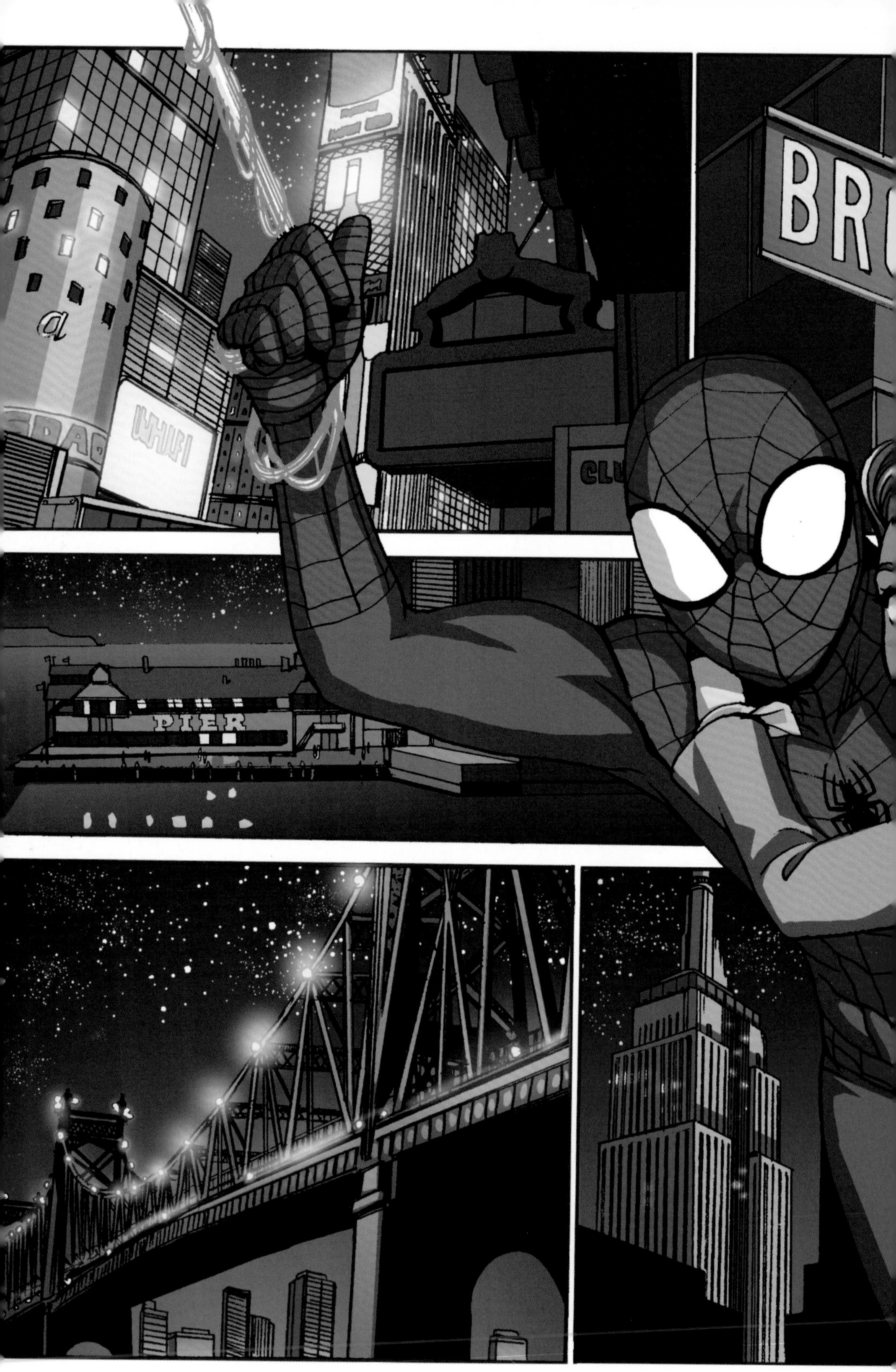
PIER

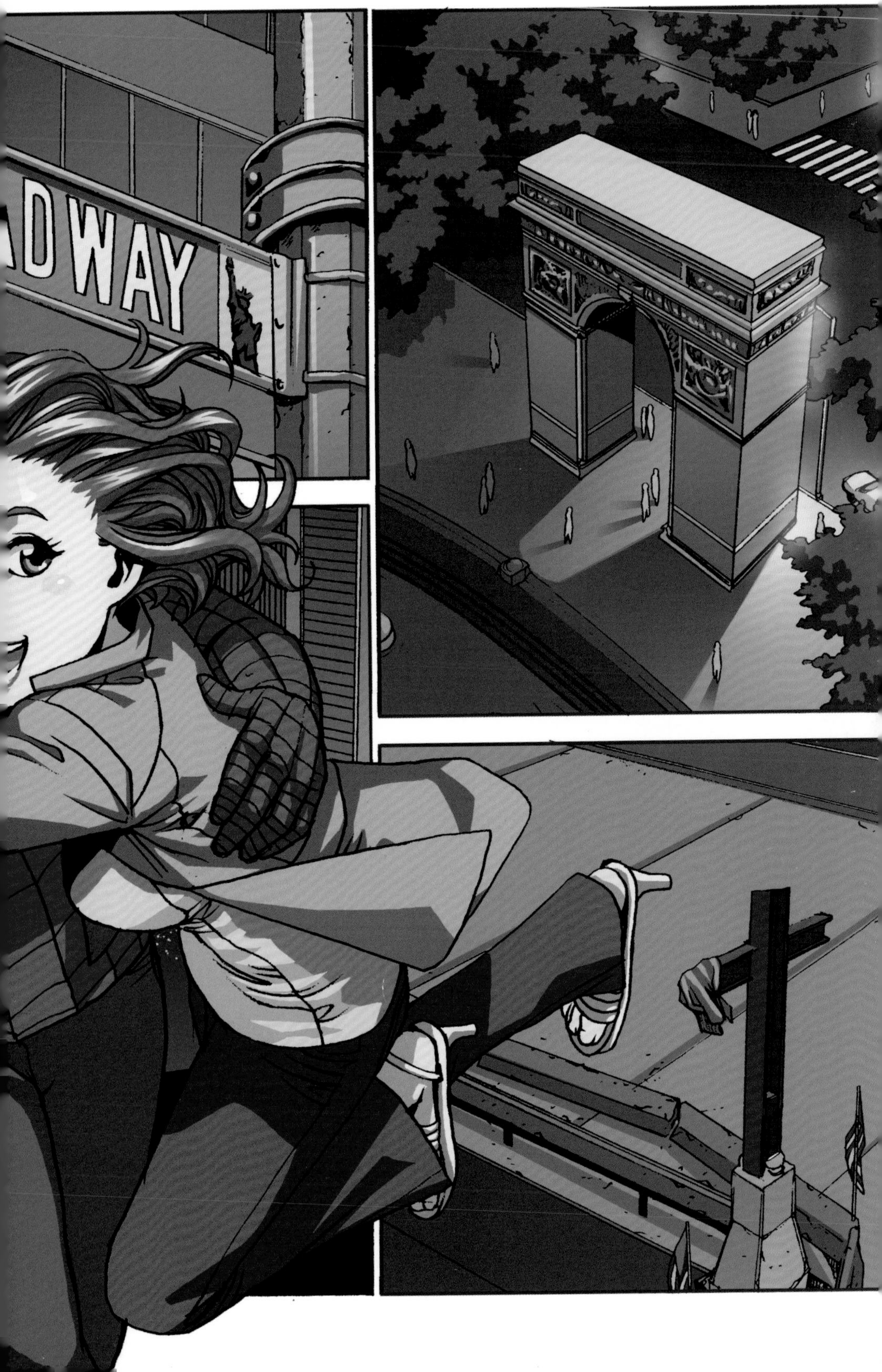
ADWAY

Wow.

That was--

I mean--

Who ever gets to see the *city* like that? You don't realize the *complexity* or the--the *beauty* of it all!

It was *over-whelming.* I--

Mary Jane? Are you okay?

Absolutely.

What's next?

Got 'em!

Here you go, sir.

Thanks, Spider-Man! Yer a real *mensch.*

Oh, hey, it was no trouble whatsoever. Just happy I could *help!*

Okay, we can get movin' again.

Anything ya *say,* Spidey! I still *owe* ya one fer savin' my *life!*

I thought you-- I mean...I figured you'd *like* this kind of--

I do! Really.

I don't know, it's just...

Well? Are you having fun?

Sure. It's nice.

But not great.

I won't stop to help people anymore. I promise.

You don't have to apologize for doing the right thing.

There's *someone else*, isn't there?

What? No.

Are you *sure?* Because it's *okay* if--

Really, it's not that at all.

I think I just...

I'm feeling kinda tired? Maybe it was all that fresh air.

Well, hey-- the night's nowhere *near* over yet!

We've still got a private tour of the *Met* and a trip to the *best* little Italian-ice stand in town. I mean, I know it's kinda *chilly* out, but--

Spider-Man.

I should probably get home.

Yeah. Okay.

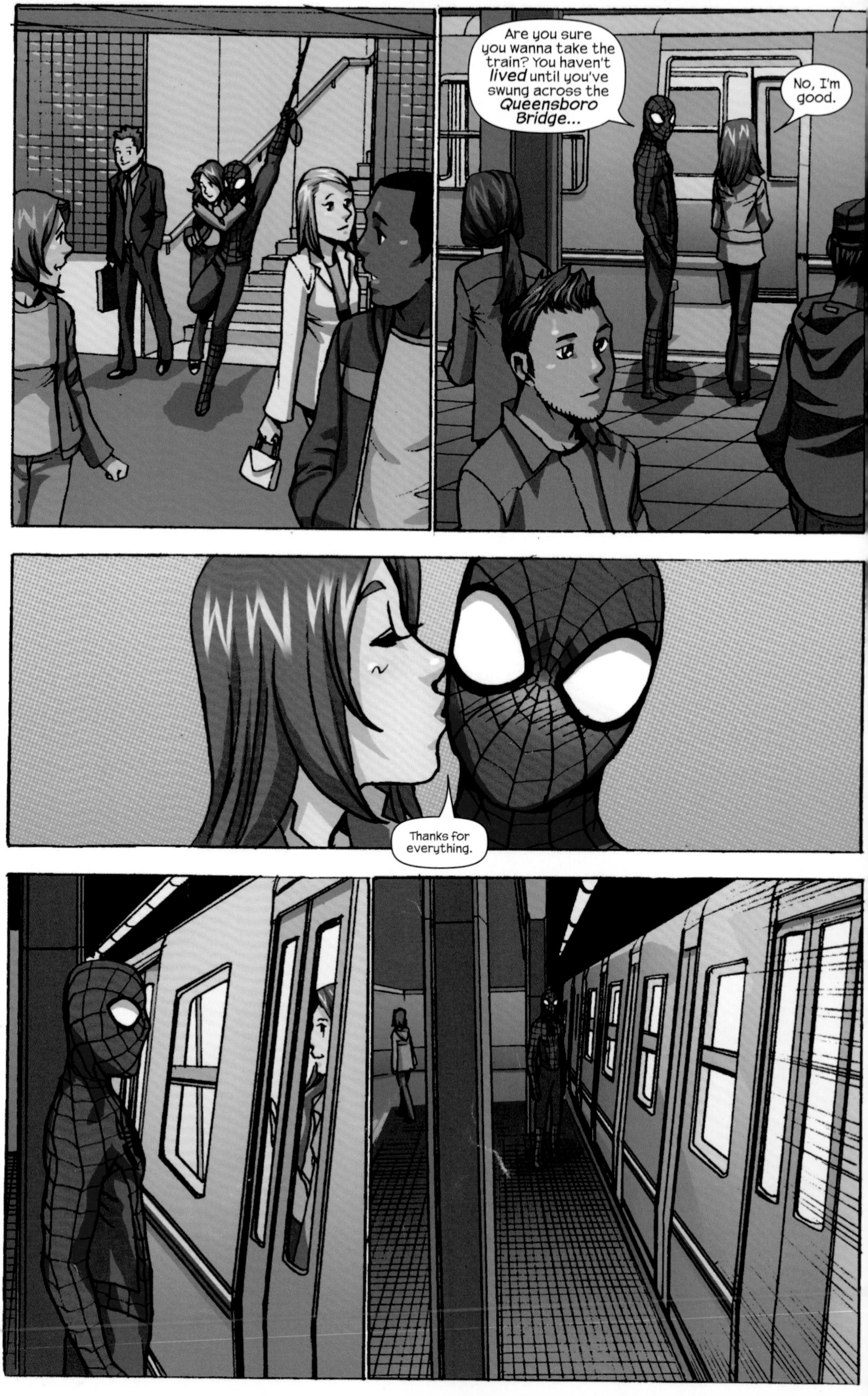
Are you sure you wanna take the train? You haven't *lived* until you've swung across the *Queensboro Bridge*...
No, I'm good.
Thanks for everything.

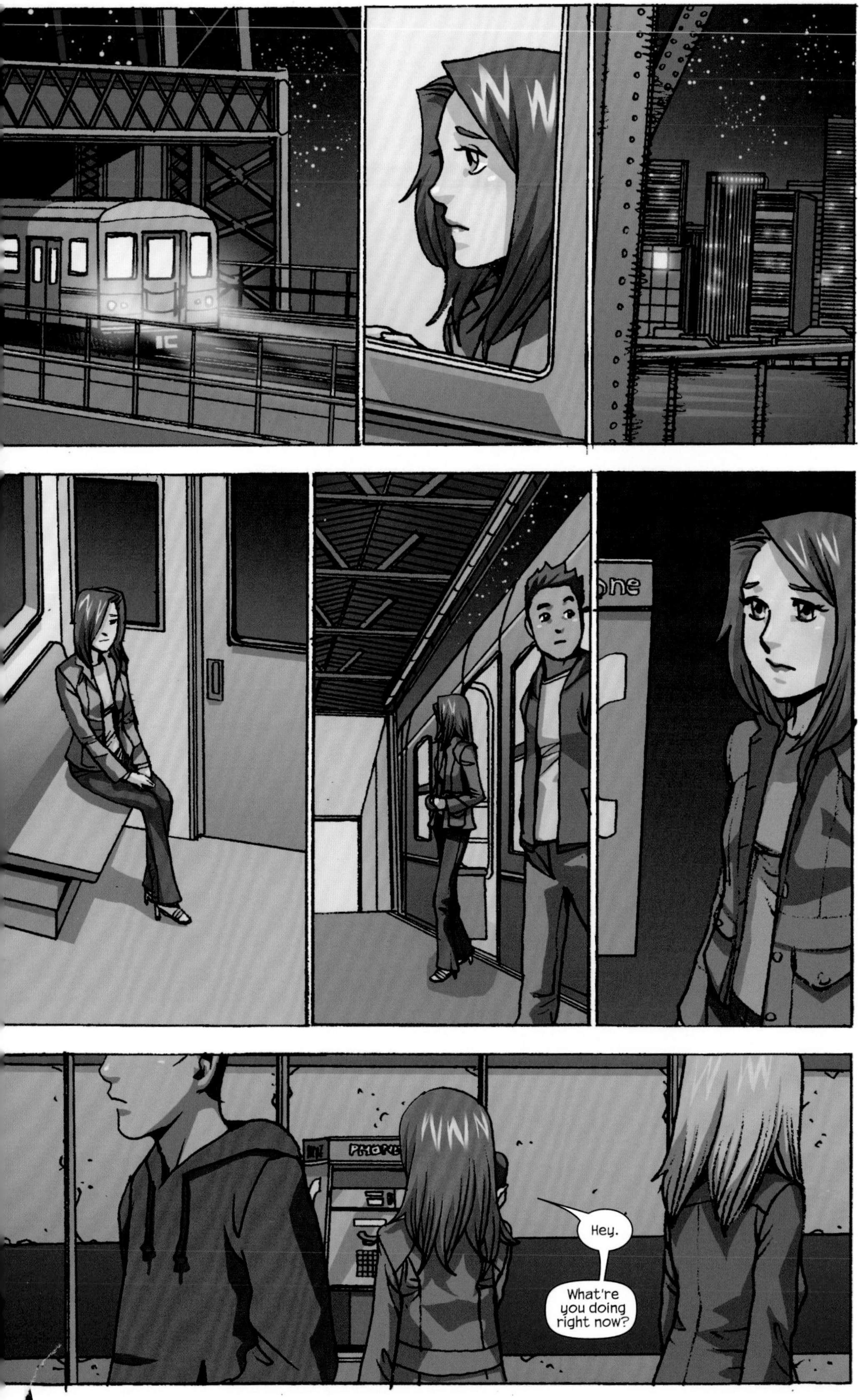
PHONE
Hey.
What're you doing right now?

We did some *really* incredible stuff, you know?

We went *swinging* around the *city!* He made this little *picnic* on a web...

...but it was...what's the word?

Fleeting?

Yeah. Fleeting. And everything else we did? *Normal-people* stuff? I hate to say it, but it was *boring.*

On our first date, *Harry* took me on a carriage ride and it was *romantic.* But with *Spider-Man?* I mean--he's Spider-Man! It's just so...

We hardly had *anything* to talk about because he *refuses* to discuss anything about his *personal* life, so it was all just *super-villains* and *mindless small talk.*

And I couldn't look into his eyes. I couldn't see if he was smiling. Or happy. Or as bored as I was or what.

It could never work between us. There's no way. Like, we could never do normal couple stuff like go out for dinner, see a movie, hang out at a party...

In *other* words...

...you *told* me so, Liz.

Well, I'm not *happy* about being right, if that makes you feel any better.

He totally *knew* I was let down, too. I feel *bad*, 'cause it's not like it was *his* fault, really...

You know, he actually *asked* me if there was some-one else.

I told him there wasn't. And that was the truth. But the whole ride home, I kept wondering...

...why you weren't with *Peter Parker?*

Don't look so surprised. I see how you *are* when you're with him.

It's like.. you're totally comfortable. You're... free.

Heck, you don't even care that anyone sees you hanging out with such a *huge nerd!*

He *is* a huge nerd, isn't he?

And he'd do *anything* for you. You *know* that, right?

What?

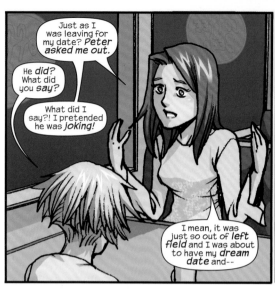

Just as I was leaving for my date? Peter *asked me out.*

He *did?* What did you *say?*

What did I say?! I pretended he was *joking!*

I mean, it was just so out of *left field* and I was about to have my *dream date* and--

Uchh. I hate myself.

And *Peter* probably hates me, too...

Hey.

You *like* Peter, don't you? As *more than a friend.*

I... yeah. I think I do.

You *know* how badly I want us to be able to hang out as *two single girls*...but...

...I've talked to him, and I'm *telling* you, MJ...you will *never* find a guy who's geeked for you the way *Peter Parker* is.

Sure, he's the biggest nerd *ever* and I can't see how any girl could actually *go* for him, but...he *cares* about you.

So, if *you* really care about *him*...

...you have to let him know how you *feel.*

Sorry, sweetie, but even if he *has* called in sick, I'm not allowed to *tell* you...

Harry!

Whoa. MJ, let's not--

Forget about all the drama between us for a sec. Have you seen *Peter*?

I couldn't reach him all *weekend*, and now I can't *find* him anywhere. Is he *okay*? Do you know?

Wow. *Relax*, MJ.

Pete's *fine*. I just saw him a little while ago. He's doing that new student *liaison* thing, showing this *girl* around--

What girl?

I wish I *knew*, but Pete's a smart guy. He's keeping her all to *himself*.

She's a real *knockout*, too. Blonde.

I think they were headed for the *school library*...

Hey! If you get her *name*, pass it along to *me*, would ya?

--so *funny*, Peter!

Don't tell me you never *heard* that one before...

Well, sure, but...not the way *you* tell it.

It's cute.

Oh! MJ. Hey.

I tried to *call* you all weekend, but your aunt said--

Yeah. Sorry about that.

So, Peter, who's your *friend*?

Oh. Right. Sorry.

This is Mary Jane Watson, my study partner.

Mary Jane...

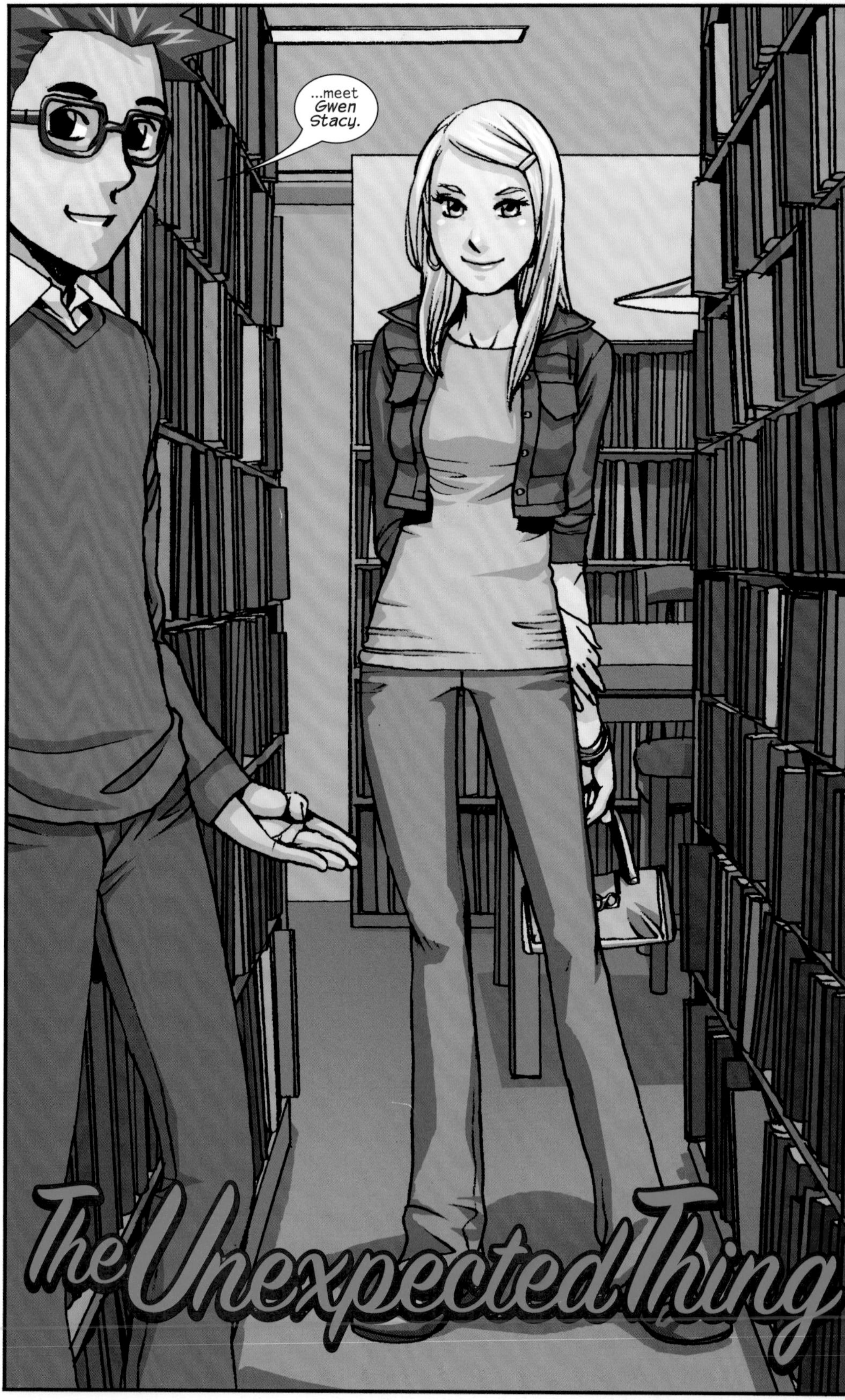
...meet Gwen Stacy.
The Unexpected Thing

Spider-Man Loves Mary Jane #6

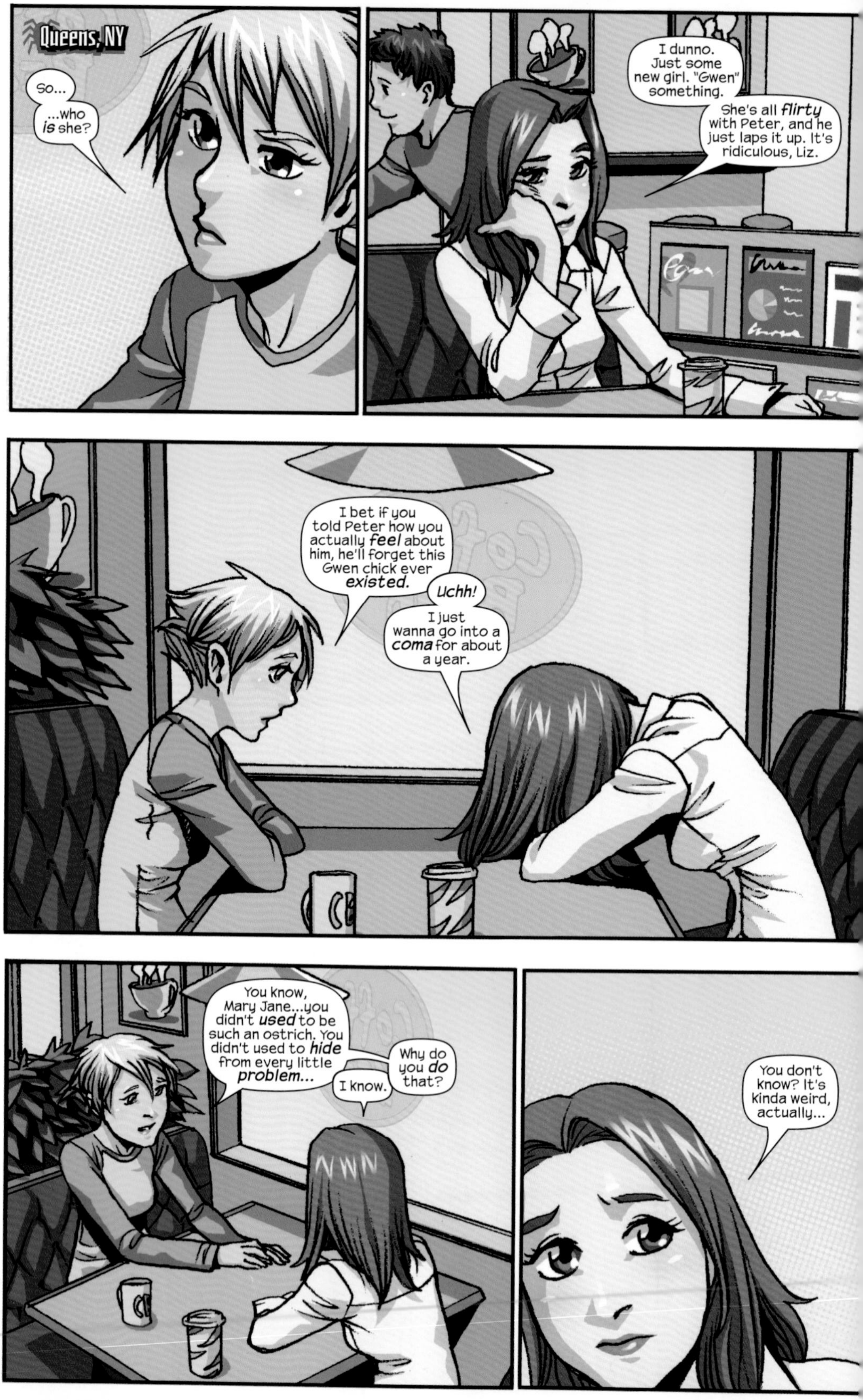
Queens, NY
So...
...who is she?
I dunno. Just some new girl. "Gwen" something.
She's all flirty with Peter, and he just laps it up. It's ridiculous, Liz.
I bet if you told Peter how you actually feel about him, he'll forget this Gwen chick ever existed.
Uchh!
I just wanna go into a coma for about a year.
You know, Mary Jane...you didn't used to be such an ostrich. You didn't used to hide from every little problem...
I know.
Why do you do that?
You don't know? It's kinda weird, actually...

"I became like that the first time I noticed Peter Parker."

Looking *very* lovely, Mary Jane. I predict a *banner day* for you, hon.

Tch. Miss Amundson...

...you say that *every* day.

VOTE AMBER ☆☆☆ FOR TREAS

ROM & JUL

Here ya go, MJ! Saved it *just for you*, gorgeous.

Hey, MJ.

Hey, Trina.

You're *welcome* to sit with us if you *want*, MJ.

I've already got a seat, but thanks.

Oh, *look* who decided to *sit* with us! We're so *special*!

You guys're my best friends. I sit with you *every day*.

Yeah, but how long's *that* gonna last, Miss Popular? Hmm?

Whatever. Spaz.

Maybe I'm dating *Flash* instead of some big-shot *senior* like you are, MJ, but if I'd actually *made* the football cheerleading squad?

I'd be, like, Midtown High *royalty*.

Two months later and she *still* isn't over it.

Yeah, Liz, what's the big deal?

Now you can sit in the bleachers and cheer for *Flash Thompson*, the *world's greatest bench-warmer!*

Watch it, Osborn. I'm *gonna* be starting varsity quarterback next year.

Yeah. *Watch* it, Harry.

So, *any*way...

I was thinking we should all go out to the *movies* tonight! Me and *Ned*, you and Flash--

--and Harry could bring whatever girl he's dating this week!

Nice one. Now who's the spaz?

I, uh, I got it.

Here you go, Mary Jane.

Oh. Thanks, um...

Peter Parker!

Hey, I can't make the field trip to the *science exhibit* thing today. You think maybe you could copy your *notes* for me?

Uh...I guess I... could... Harry...

C'mon, Liz. I have to *tell* you something.

So *spill* it already!

Nuh-uh. Come with me.

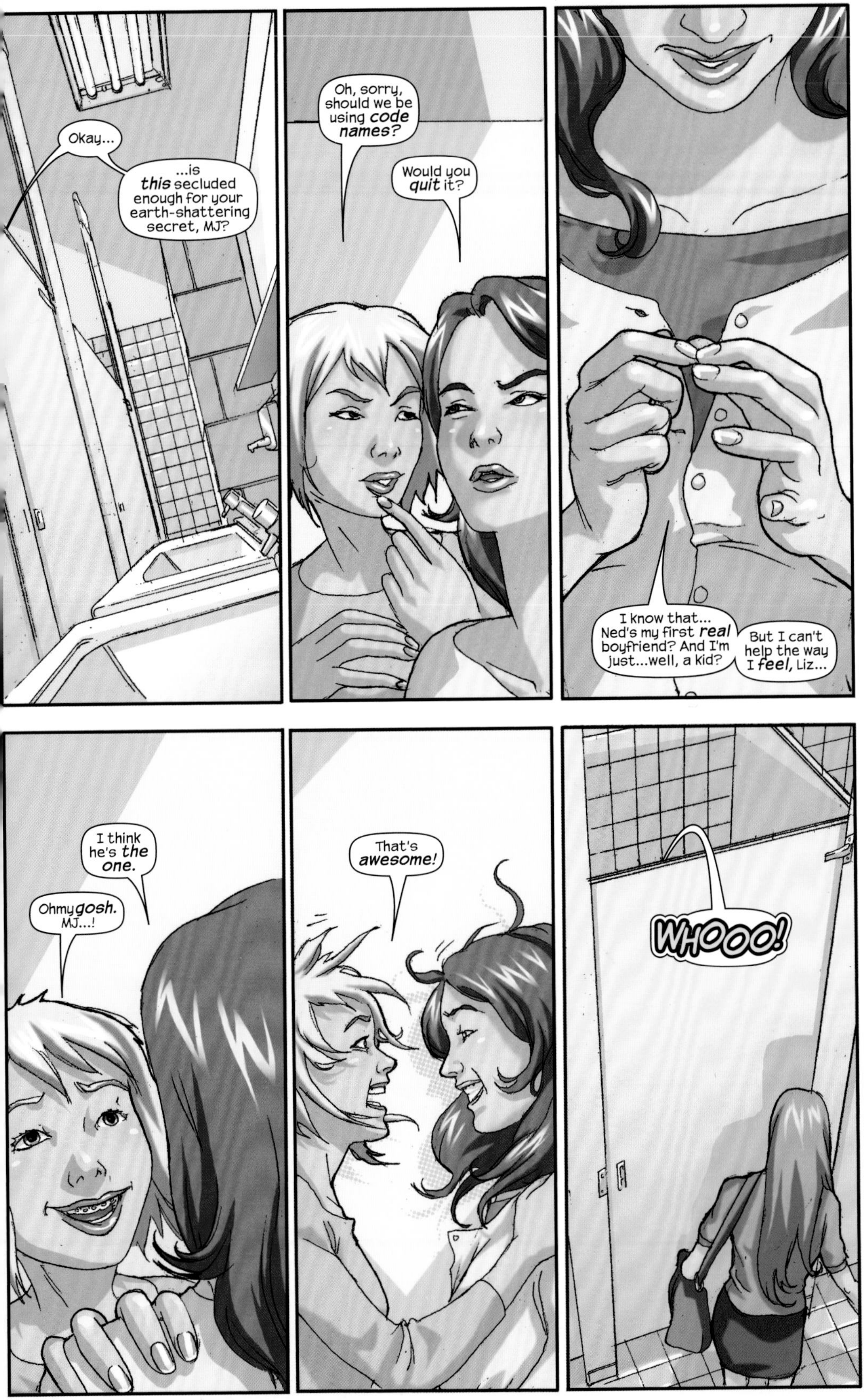
Okay...
...is this secluded enough for your earth-shattering secret, MJ?
Oh, sorry, should we be using code names?
Would you quit it?
I know that... Ned's my first real boyfriend? And I'm just...well, a kid?
But I can't help the way I feel, Liz...
I think he's the one.
Ohmygosh. MJ...!
That's awesome!
WHOOO!

CHEMISTRY

I didn't think you'd *want* me to. You know, in front of your new friends?

Frankly, I'm surprised you even *recognized* me from last year. Amazing how quickly someone can *change*, huh?

You haven't *changed*, Jessica. You're just...

A freak?

Down-hearted.

You didn't say hi to me at lunch.

Right.

Well...I hate to *break* it to you, Mary Jane, but this is who I *am* now.

Anyway... those guys think of you as a *plastic*, so...

...thanks, I guess, for not saying anything.

Hrm.

She just needs to *cheer up*...

Who needs to cheer up?

NED!

Where've you *been* all day? I looked *all over* for you!

Yeah, I know, I--

Oh! We're going to the *movies* tonight!

Mary Jane...

I asked Flash and Liz and Harry to come along.

I hope you don't *mind*, but it's just they're my *friends*, you know. And you haven't really gotten to *know* them--

Mary Jane.

Stop.

Ned, are you okay?

Look, MJ, I don't know how to *tell* you this, so I'll just--

I ran into *Betty* last night at the mall.

Betty?

I hadn't really seen her since she had to *drop out,* you know? But we got to *talking* last night, and I realized...

...I still care about her.

Ned, what are you--

What are you saying?

Ohmygosh.

You're a *great girl,* Mary Jane. This isn't about you. It's just...

...bad timing.

Look, I gotta go.

I'm sorry.

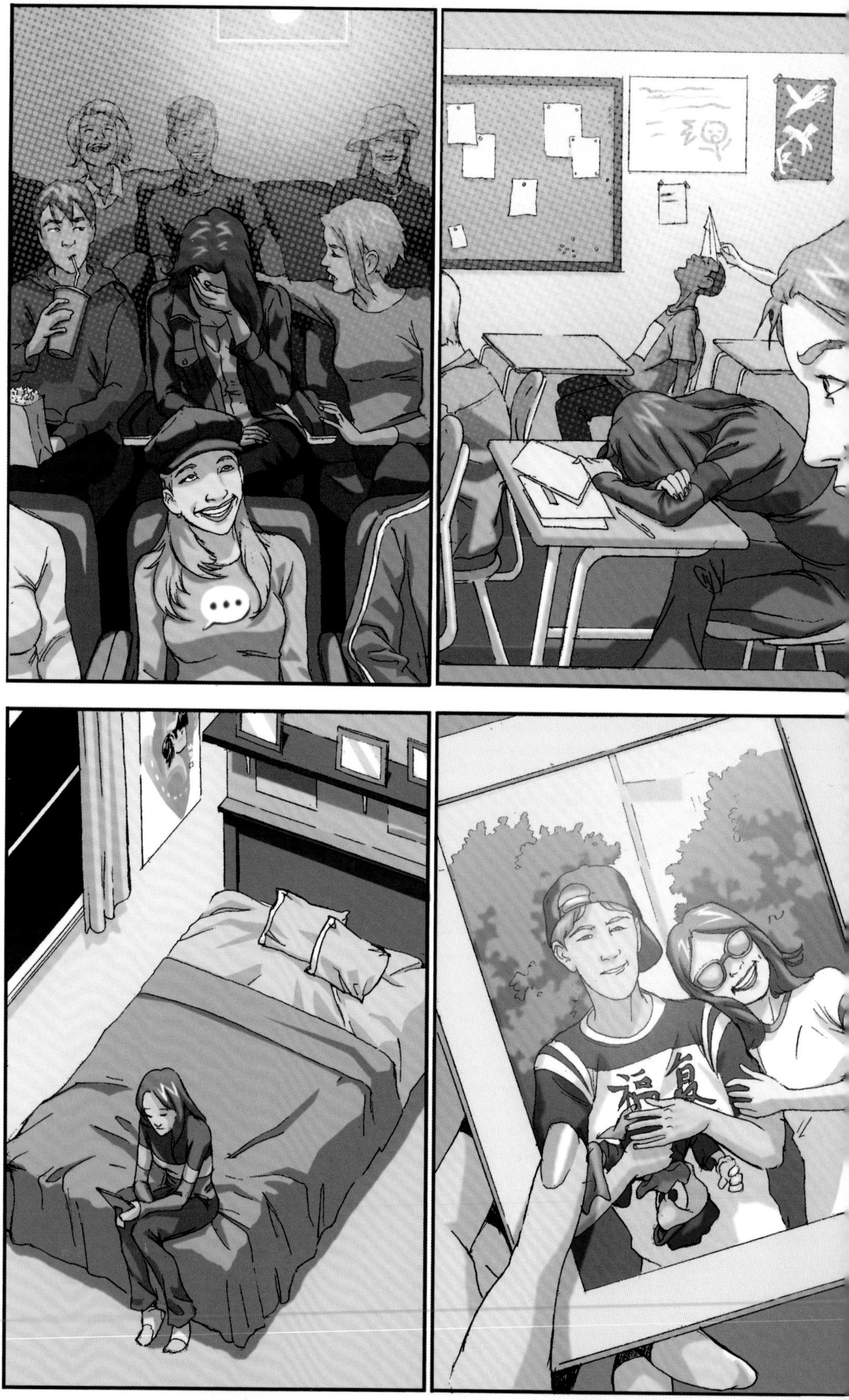
...

Now I know. *This* is what it feels like.

To be unwanted.

Alone.

To realize that everything that blossoms...

...eventually withers and *fades*.

I've gotta admit, Mary Jane, when you called and said you wanted to *hang out* with me, I was pretty skeptical.

I thought you were gonna try to help "fix" me or something. 'Cause, y'know, *everyone* wants to "fix" me.

Whatever. They just don't understand you.

Us.

It's like, one second you're you and then *life* comes along and just...

It changes you. You know?

Yeah. Yeah, totally.

Oh, come onnn. You haven't smiled in over a week! Something's gotta cheer you up.

Forget it, Liz.

I don't wanna be cheered up.

Lies. Everyone wants to be cheered up.

Yeah, c'mon, MJ. Who needs Ned Leeds?

Okay, you're one hundred percent not helping.

Go.

What's the point of being happy, anyway? I'll just meet another guy and get all hurt again when he dumps me.

Listen to me, MJ...

...I dump girls all the time, and they all get over me.

I mean, sure, it takes 'em, like, months most of the time, but--

And here I thought Flash was the big dummy.

Wha--?

Depart!

Sorry, MJ. They *mean* well, but...

...well, they're *boys*.

You should *see* this guy, Harry. He's, like, *super strong* and can crawl around the cage like a *spider!* He's *unreal!*

Dude, you *gotta* know that wrestling stuff's *fake*, right?

Fake? What're you *talkin'* about?

Pete! Man, what's *goin' on?* I never got your *notes* from that exhibit.

Yeah, uh... sorry about that, Harry, but...

...I didn't *take* any notes.

You didn't--? But you're *Peter Parker!* You *always* take notes!

That paper's due *Friday!* I don't know what I'm gonna *do...*

Puny Parker here screwed ya up, so *he's* gonna write your paper. Ain't that right?

Yeah? Are you gonna *make* me, Bench Brain?

Flash, knock it off. It's *my* problem--not his.

So, what's...all this?

All what?

I don't *believe* this! I finally woulda *trashed* his nerdy butt!

The *eyeliner*? All the *doom and gloom*?

I mean...what, are you gonna write *bad poetry* now or something?

I wouldn't expect you to understand.

Hff...

Okay. Look at me. You *may* have noticed that I get bent outta *shape* every once in a while.

I *express* my feelings, and then I'm my usual, merry self. *That's* healthy. That's all good.

But this...? I mean...

...what is it you're trying to *be*?

And *here's* a story for your *"believe it or not"* files, viewers...

Amateur video captured what *appears* to be a *costumed* vigilante--swinging on a *rope!*

Police say this mysterious figure *apprehended* a man wanted in connection with *several crimes,* including the death of *Forest Hills* resident Benjamin Parker--

--and then *took off* into the night like, quote, "an *urban Tarzan,"* unquote.

Wouldn't that be a *swinging* good time, Amber?

Haha, you don't have to *sway* me, Brock!

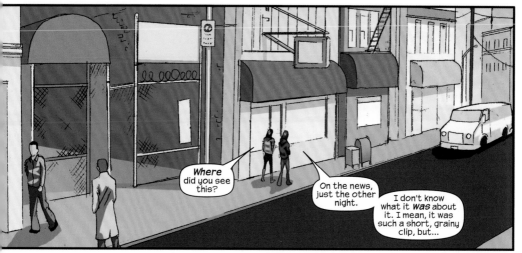

Where did you see this?

On the news, just the other night.

I don't know what it **was** about it. I mean, it was such a short, grainy clip, but...

...I wanted so badly to **be** there.

Sounds like it was cool.

Makes me wonder, MJ...you're talking about something you *enjoyed watching*...

...but you *look* like you're going to a *funeral*.

I'm in mourning.

Wow.

Mary Jane, you have to listen to me...

WHOA!

The heck *was* that...?

UHH!

AAAAA--!

NO!

NUHH!

...nnn...

C'mon... what's your *beef*, man?

You don't *take* what doesn't *belong* to you.

Hold it! Police!

Hands above your head!

Take it easy... these two guys *stole* that car.

We *know,* genius! They've been under *surveillance!*

We were about to *follow* 'em to their *chop shop* till *you* showed up! Now the whole *operation's* a loss!

Yeah? What do *you* know about *loss?*

Do you know what it's like to have someone in your life *one* day and the next thing you know they're *gone*?

Look, I don't know what you're talking about, and I don't exactly *care.*

You leave the police work to *us,* you under-stand me?

We don't *want* ya, and we sure don't *need* ya.

Fine.

Hey...

You can't just leave!

Get back here!

Uh... wow.

I take it that's the guy.

Mary Jane?

Mary Jane.

The Origin Thing PART 1

Spider-Man Loves Mary Jane #7

Hold it, hold it, **hold** it.

You said you were gonna tell me how you started dealing with your problems by **not** dealing with them 'cause of **something** to do with Peter Parker.

That's not really what I **do**, Liz--

Is that or is that not the **gist** of what you set out to tell me?

Yeah...

Well, my dear, darling MJ, I think you need to get your **head** checked, 'cause **I** just heard the story of how you started going all **ga-ga** over **Spider-Man**.

No, I know. But the Spidey stuff and the Peter stuff...it's related, kinda.

Okay, whatever. But at **this** rate, Peter and that **Gwen** chick? They'll be **married** by the time you finish.

Did you know that with every passing day you become just a little bit **crueler**?

Yes.

So, okay...so, I saw Spidey **in person** for the first time ever, and, as I'm sure you **remember**...

"...I came to look at him as a sort of *kindred spirit.*"

Excuse me. Just *what* do you think you're *doing?*

That's *school property.*

Oh.

Like I'm supposed to *care?*

MR. J. LIMKE
COUNSELOR

Good *morning,*
Miss
Watson.

I see you're
trying out a
new *look.*

HANG
IN
THERE!

The
world sure
is *changing,*
isn't it?

One day everything's fine, and then the *next* day, some guy's scaling skyscrapers and firing *webs* out of his hands.

You were so sure you *understood* how the world works, but now...I mean, you *have* to question it, don't you? How could this happen? Why?

So, what do you do?

Well...you get *used* to it.

The truth is, even though we may never come to *understand* these upheavals in our world, we *do* eventually come to *grips* with them.

We adapt. We come to *accept* these things as a part of our lives.

But...if we accept it, doesn't that kinda mean we've taught ourselves not to *feel* as much?

It means we've *grown*, Miss Watson.

Coffee Bean

Obsessing over a celebrity isn't what I'd call the *healthiest* sort of rebound.

I've had a *few* girls do that after dating me. It's never pretty.

Liz, are you *sure* about this?

Yeah, but Harry...

...for the first time since Ned broke up with her, MJ's been in a mood that at least *resembles* happiness. If that's because of the *wrestler guy,* then...whatever. It's fine.

It's *temporary.* Fast-forward a couple months and she'll be into someone else entirely.

And normal.

The radio says it's gonna be *over!* Let's just *go* already!

Did you just become a *six-year-old* or something?

We have to wait for *MJ,* knucklehead.

Wait for me for *what?*

Finally. I *hate* the train...

Sourpuss.

NOW can you tell me what we're doing?

YES!

Yes, yes, yes!

Hurry *up*, MJ, or you're gonna--

Aww, man...!

They didn't say it's over yet! How'd we *miss* it?

Could *someone* please tell me what it is we were supposed to have--?

WHOA!

I'm **not** letting you get away with what you've done!

Is that right?

Your persistence is most *impressive*, Spider-Man, but I *really* must be on my--!

URK!

You're not going *anywhere*, ugly!

Care to make a bet?

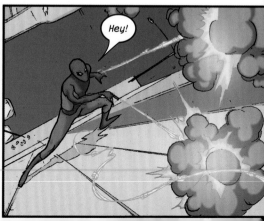

Hey!

What's **wrong** with you? What if those people down there were **hurt**?

I promise you I could **live** with it.

But **you**, on the other hand...

NO!

≶UNNH!≶

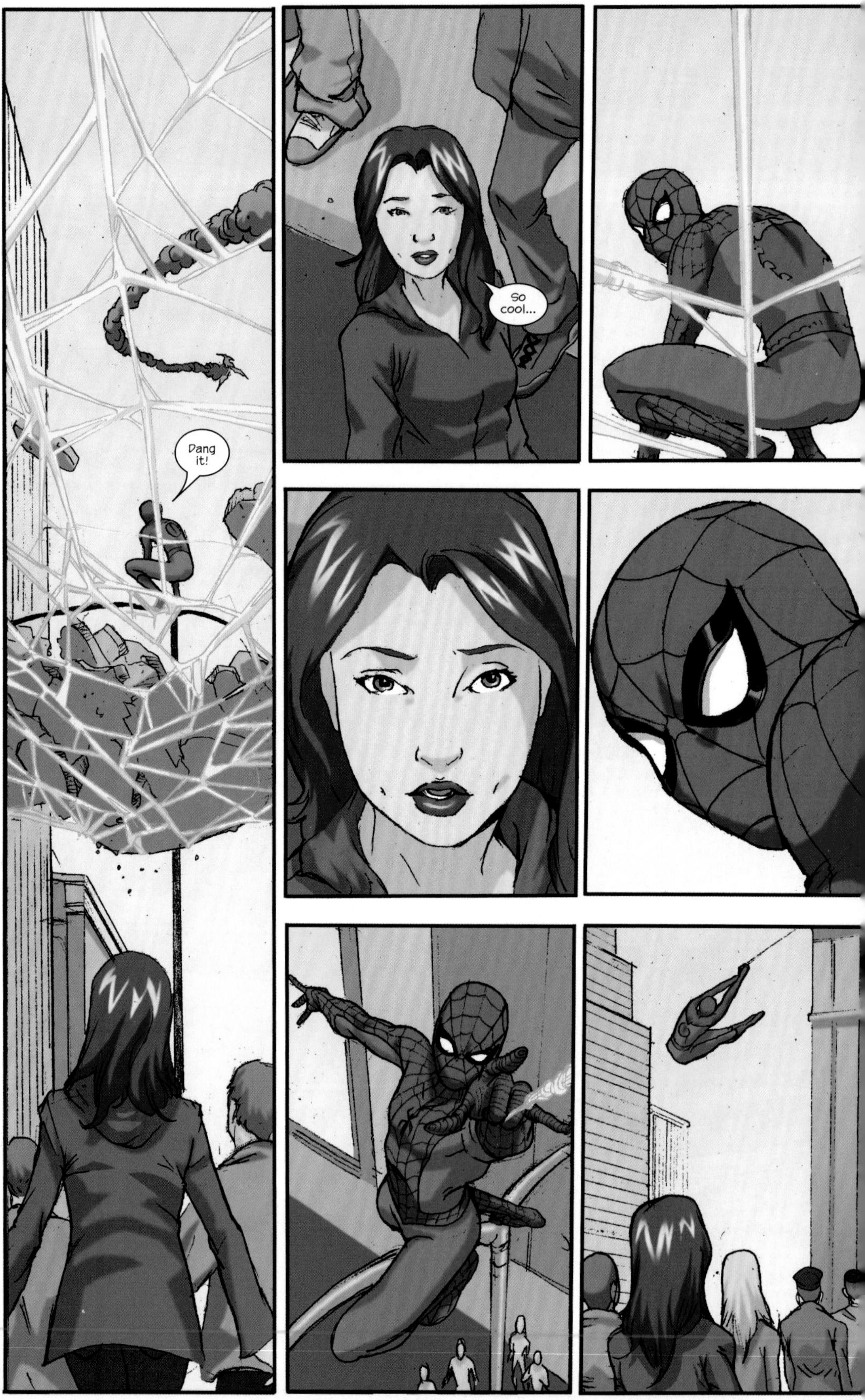
Dang it!
So cool...

So, was that cool or was that *cool?*

It was. It was very cool.

You're *welcome...!*

That's us.

You sure you don't want to go to the *Bean* with us, MJ?

I'm pretty wiped. Guess I've had enough fun for one day.

Thanks, though.

Tch.
So silly...

Haha!

Mary Jane?

Ned.

You look, ah...

Wow. You really look *different*.

Um... Well, I saw you and just thought I'd say, y'know...

Come on. *One* of these cars is empty...

You... take care of yourself, okay?

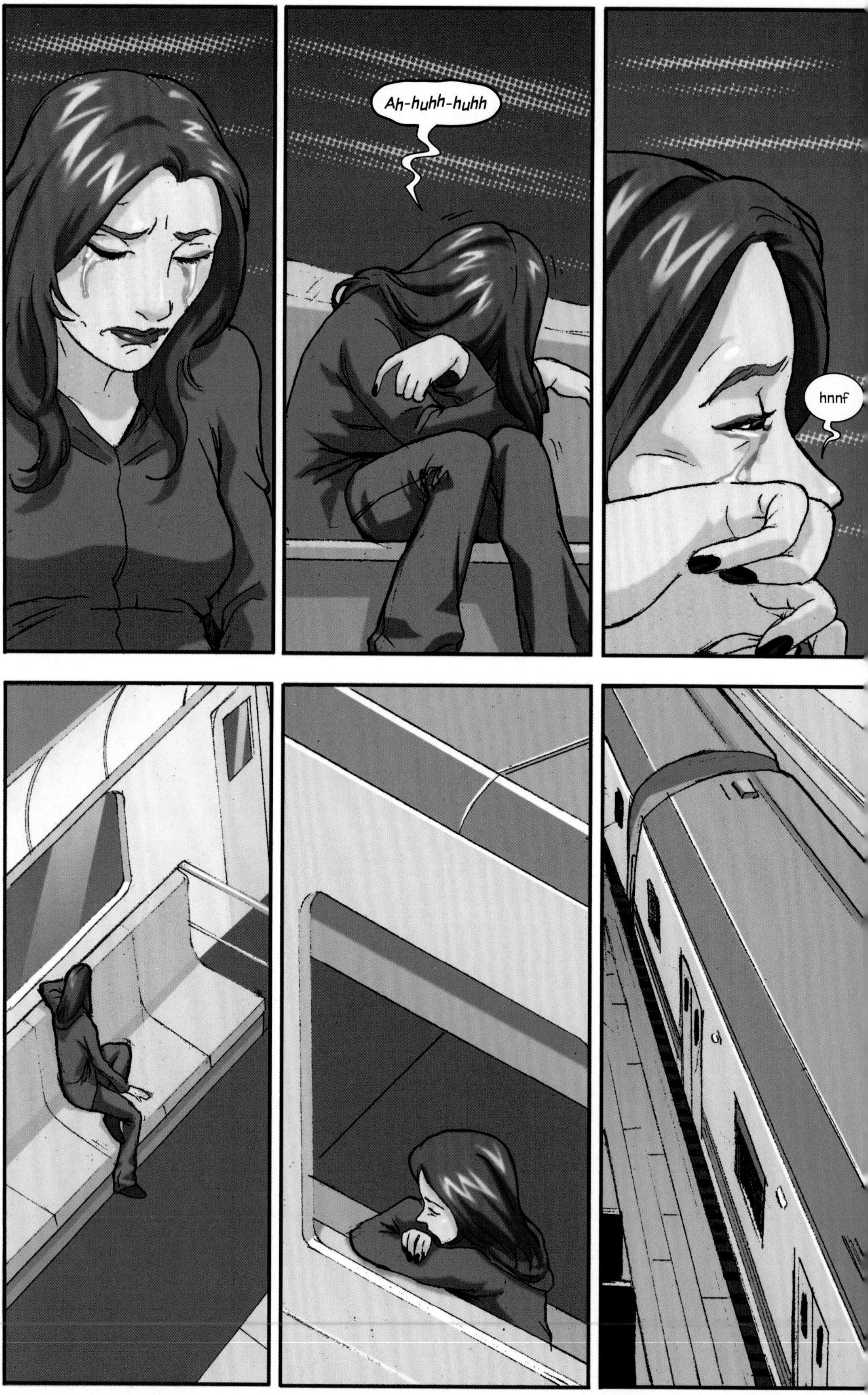
Ah-huhh-huhh
hnnf

Parker!

Hey, Parker! Where's the *funeral?*

Aww, whassamatter? Are you gonna *cry?*

Look at him go. I think he's really gonna go cry.

Geez, Flash. Could you be *any* more insensitive?

Oh, whatever. Not *my* fault he can't hack it.

You didn't hear what *happened* last week, did you?

What? Did he break a *beaker?*

It can't be *that* bad... can it?

It's like I *saw* him and all of a sudden he's breaking up with me all *over* again!

I just don't think I was ever *meant* to be happy, Jessica.

Okay... this has to stop.

What has to--?

All of it. The moping. The black clothes. The mascara...

You're *Mary Jane Watson.* You're the popular, happy party girl that all the other girls *wish* they could be.

Are you...? You're trying to cheer me up?

Face it, Mary Jane.

This isn't *you.*

What's that mean? Somehow my feelings aren't *real* enough? I'm too *shallow* to know what *despair* is?

No, I'm just *saying*--

Mary Jane?!

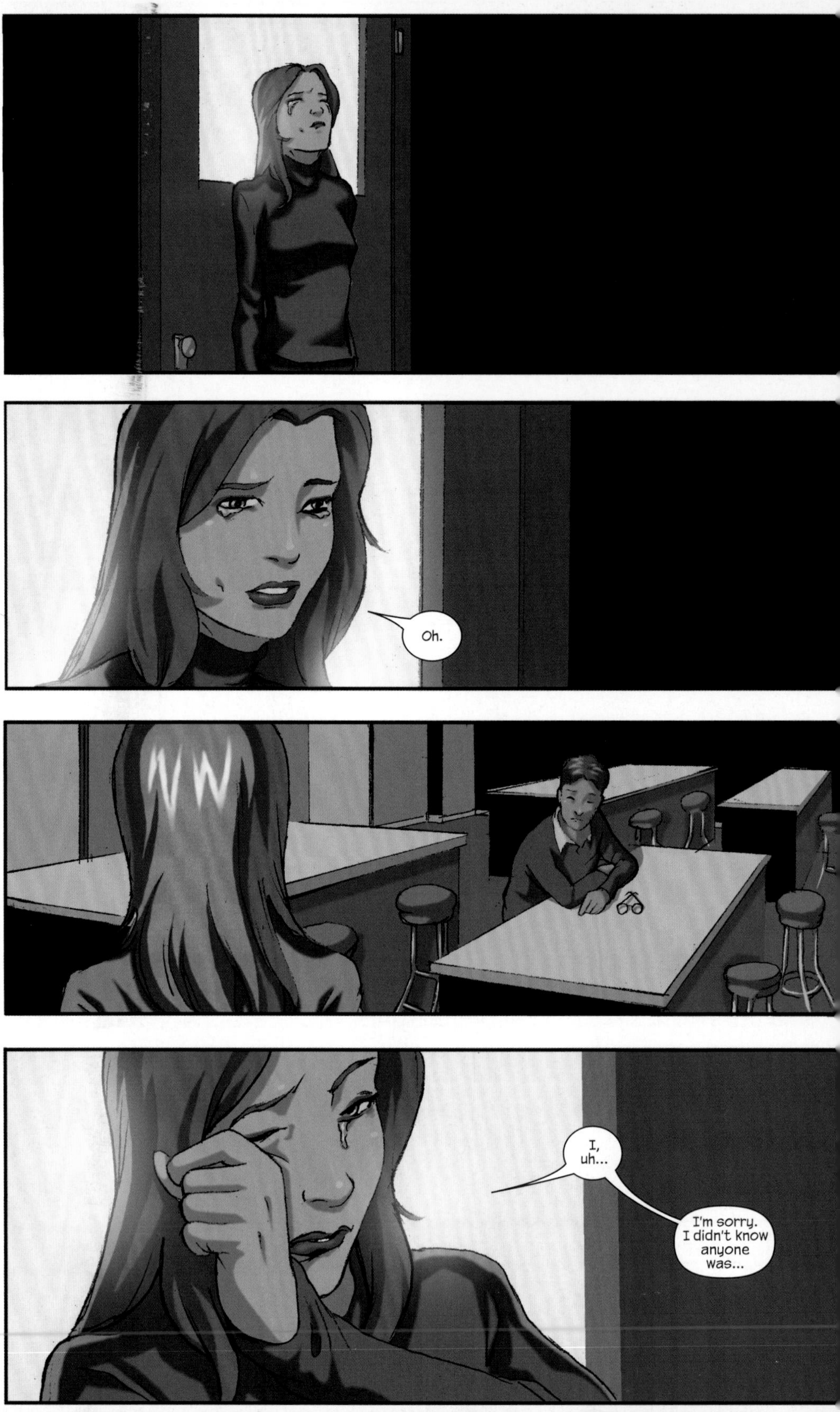
Oh.
I, uh...
I'm sorry. I didn't know anyone was...

Are you okay?

Not really.

Are you?

It's my uncle. He, ah...

He was the kindest man to ever walk this earth. Never selfish, never cruel...

He had me and my aunt to provide for and worked to the *bone* just to scrape by, but he never complained, *not once*...

Benjamin Parker.

I'm sorry for your loss.

"The way he looked, all alone in that room...it's like what Mr. Limke was trying to tell me, you know?"

"His whole world was just...torn apart."

The man who raised him was dead, and there *I* was, crying my eyes out and basically changing my entire *outlook* on life over a *breakup.*

I mean, how *trivial,* right?

So now, instead of *wallowing* in despair, you *hide* from it.

Basically. Yeah.

Mary Jane...

I love you, but you're *stupid.*

You can't *do* that, MJ! It's not *healthy!*

You have to *deal* with your problems.

I know. I know.

And I think you *know* where you should start.

You *have* to tell Peter how you *feel* about him. You have to do it before it's *too late.*

Hey, you two!

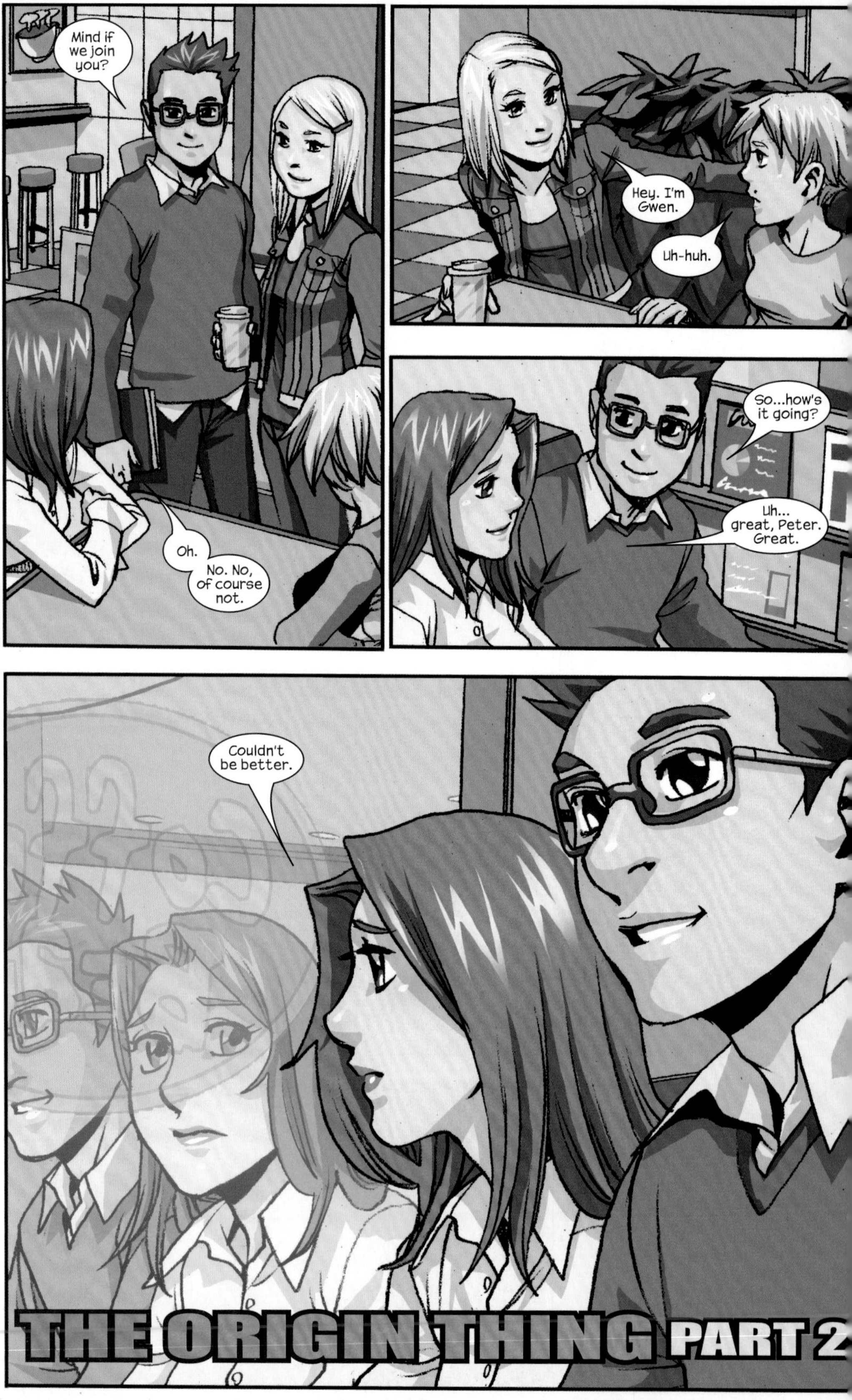
Mind if we join you?
Oh.
No. No, of course not.
Hey. I'm Gwen.
Uh-huh.
So...how's it going?
Uh... great, Peter. Great.
Couldn't be better.
THE ORIGIN THING PART 2

Spider-Man Loves Mary Jane #8

...so, since the hormone that tells you you're hungry *also* boosts your *memory*, there's *some* argument *against* studying on a full stomach.

Hmm...I dunno, Peter. If my tummy's growling, I can't focus on *anything.*

No, I agree. It's totally *counter-intuitive.* But it's what I read...

Then I think you read *way* too much.

But I also think it's cute.

Uh--

Oh, hey! Look who it is.

Hi, Mary Jane!

Peter. Gwen. Hey.

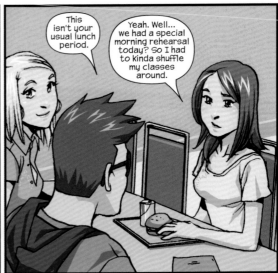

This isn't your usual lunch period.

Yeah. Well... we had a special morning rehearsal today? So I had to kinda shuffle my classes around.

Oh, that's *right*--you're starring in the *play!* Twelfth Night, right?

Peter told me about it. He's so proud of you.

So...

You're not practicing your lines?

No...

Well, it's just--

I mean, you're so *popular*. You were just *Homecoming Queen*, and *everyone* says they really *like* you, so I figured, you know, you'd be sitting with *some*--

Hey, Peter and I are going to go catch a *twilight show* after school. You should come with.

Y-yeah. Absolutely.

I can't. I have rehearsals again tonight.

Mm. Well, *that* stinks...

O my poor brother! and so perchance he may--

STOP!

Stop, stop, stop, stop, *stop*, stop, STOP.

Oh, this should be good.

Where *are* you right now, Mary Jane?

I'm-- I'm right here...?

Exactly. And *that's* why you're *ruining my play.*

You're *supposed* to be filled with *dread* and *remorse!*

Mr. Tiplady--

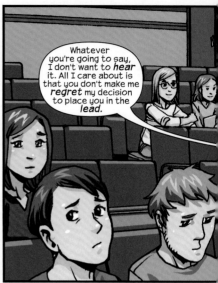

Whatever you're going to say, I don't want to *hear* it. All I care about is that you don't make me *regret* my decision to place you in the *lead.*

Now: let's get you into character.

You've just lost your twin brother--your *everything*--to the sea.

He's *gone,* leaving you with *nothing.*

You are *completely.* And *utterly.* Alone.

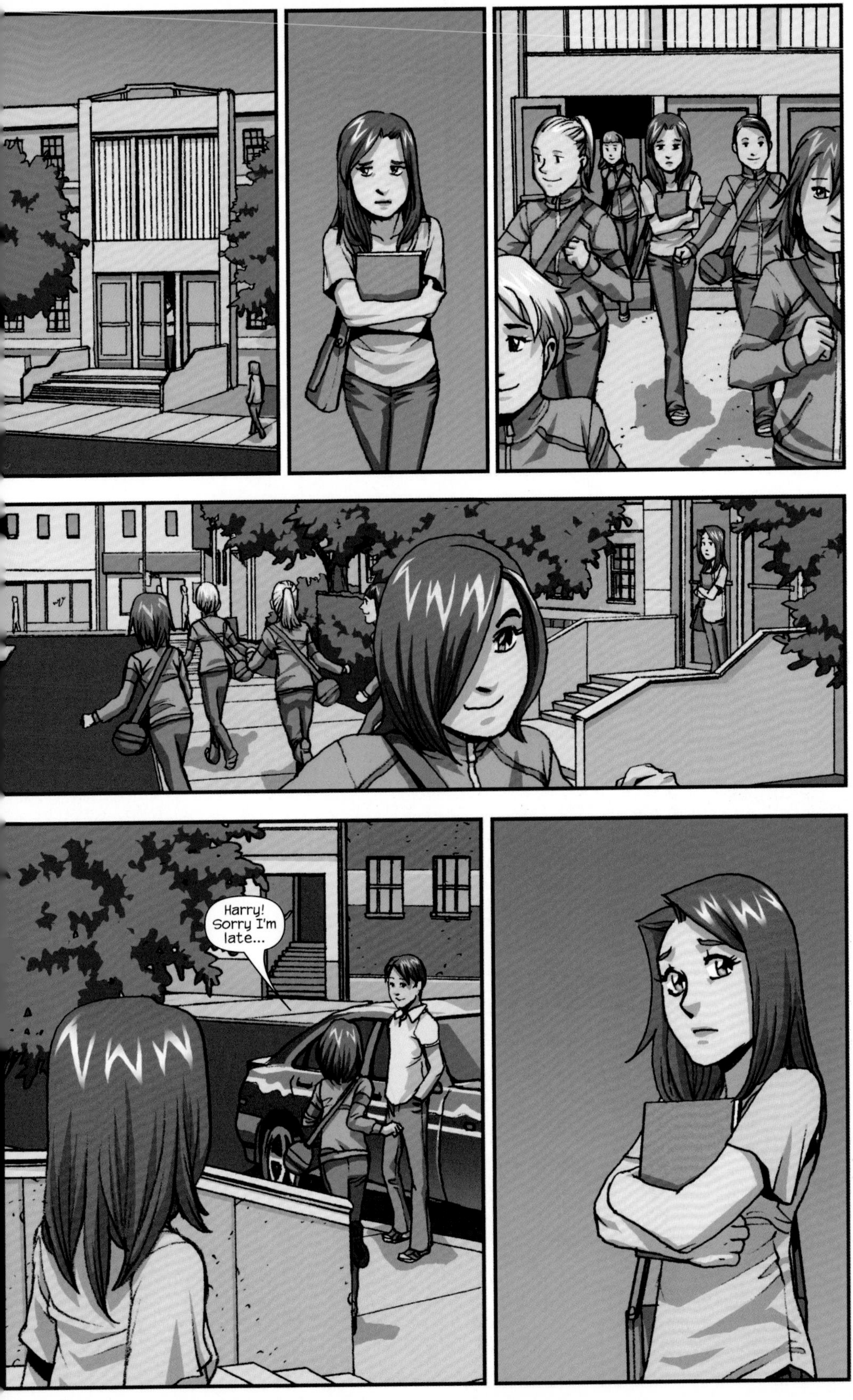
Harry! Sorry I'm late...

The Next Day...

See ya soon, Harry.

MJ. Hey.

Hey.

You're, uh... you're not gonna get all--

No. Absolutely not. I'm okay.

Really? 'Cause the *last* time I had a girlfriend, you--

Look, I'm *over* you, okay? The *least* you could do is get over *yourself*.

Wow. How very...Liz of you.

I'm sorry. That was...

Everything all right?

Yeah.

Well, no, but... I wouldn't even know where to *start*, so...

I'm cool with you, though. You know.

Here. You look like you need this...

It's a conspiracy.

Uh-huh.

Harry's dating Trish Bollinger, Peter and that *Gwen* girl are all buddy-buddy, *Flash* just went out with another girl from *your* cheer squad...

I even saw those two dweebs who used to play *pranks* on me with girlfriends.

But I guess, you know, it's like you were *hoping* it would be.

It is?

Yeah! We're both totally *single* now! "Best friends on the prowl," right?

Um... MJ...?

You're not. Tell me you're not.

Not *exactly*, no, but Flash and I were talking about maybe--

Flash?

Flash who broke your heart at *Homecoming*? Flash who'd rather beat on *Peter Parker* than be my *friend*?

So he *isn't* seeing Liana?

Well, kinda, but it's not like they're *exclusive* or anything.

What can I say?

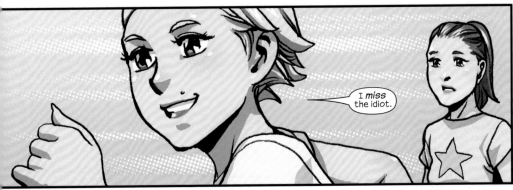

I *miss* the idiot.

Yes!

This fellow is wise enough to play the fool; And to do that well craves a kind of wit: He must observe their mood on whom he jests, The quality of persons, and the time--

You're totally talking about me, aren't you?

You!

What are you *doing*?

Um...

Not... stalking you...?

Seriously, I'm just...nosing around, sorta.

Looking for someone.

You're gonna keep *looking* at me like that until I spill the *beans,* aren't you?

Yeah. You definitely are.

There's this new bad guy going around *stealing* stuff. Calls himself the *Looter.*

Clever, I know.

Well, anyway, it's sorta *embarrassing,* but...

You can't catch the guy.

Well, I *can*-- I just *haven't* yet.

But I'm *pretty* sure, based on what I've been able to piece together, that the Looter's from *Midtown High.*

What, like a *student?*

Student or faculty, yeah.

Anyway...

So, um... how's stuff and... ...stuff?

Yeah, wow, I haven't seen you since we, uh...

Yeah.

You know, I hope--

I hope you're *cool* with--

Yeah. Yeah, totally. It wasn't the greatest idea in the *first* place.

Not that I didn't have *fun* with you or--

No. No, I understand. You're right.

But there's no reason we can't be *friends*, right? Like...hang out and stuff?

Yeah. I'd like that.

I'd *really* like that, actually.

MJ? You okay?

Oh, it's just...stuff, you know.

Well, hey...if you need someone to *talk* to...

Maybe after school?

Wow. I could get in so much *trouble* for being up here...

Not as much trouble as *I'd* be in if you fell off the roof of the *high school*, so, um...

Oh. Right. Thanks.

Okay! So, tell Dr. Spidey what's on your mind.

Look, I made you a *hammock* to lay on and everything!

Ohmygosh. Such a dork.

Well, "Dr. Spidey"...

...I guess it's just that I've been feeling kinda...

...well...

...lonely.

It's, like... everyone's *dating* someone. *Everyone.*

And, you know, there *is* a guy I like, but...it's been kinda *weird* between us, and now...

...there's *another girl* in his life. And, I mean, I *guess* I could still pursue him...

...but what if I'm just coming between him and a really great relationship?

Well...as much as I'd like to see you *happy*, Mary Jane...

...I think you just hit the nail on the head.

But I still really *care* about him.

Who says you can't? Just because you're not *romantically* involved...

Look, the *important* thing to remember is, as long as you have friends who love you, there's no *reason* to feel alone.

Being single's hardly the end of the world.

Thanks for listening, Spidey.

Hey, I'll take you over Doc Ock or the Sandman *any* day.

And thanks for your advice. I mean it.

I better get to rehearsal. See ya!

Boy...

...that Harry Osborn is one *lucky guy*...

Try this. Does this taste **weird** to you?

Hmm. Yeah, actually, it's--

What **is** that? It's awfully familiar. It tastes like...

Oh! I know! It tastes like you're trying to **change the subject.**

Now, did you **talk** to Peter or **not?**

I--

Liz, it's just not a good **idea** right now. I could be getting in the way of a really great **thing** between Peter and Gwen.

Well, yeah! That's kinda the **point,** isn't it?

I'm just saying...being single is **hardly** the end of the world.

What the heck are you **talking** about? You like Peter. Peter likes you. It isn't even the **tiniest** bit complicated.

You need to **do** something about it.

I *get* it, Liz. You just don't want me feeling *left out* when you're dating *Flash* and I'm not dating *anyone*.

It's very *sweet* of you, but--

But I'm not.

What?

I'm not dating Flash. And I'm not gonna.

Really? But I thought--

Can I talk to you?

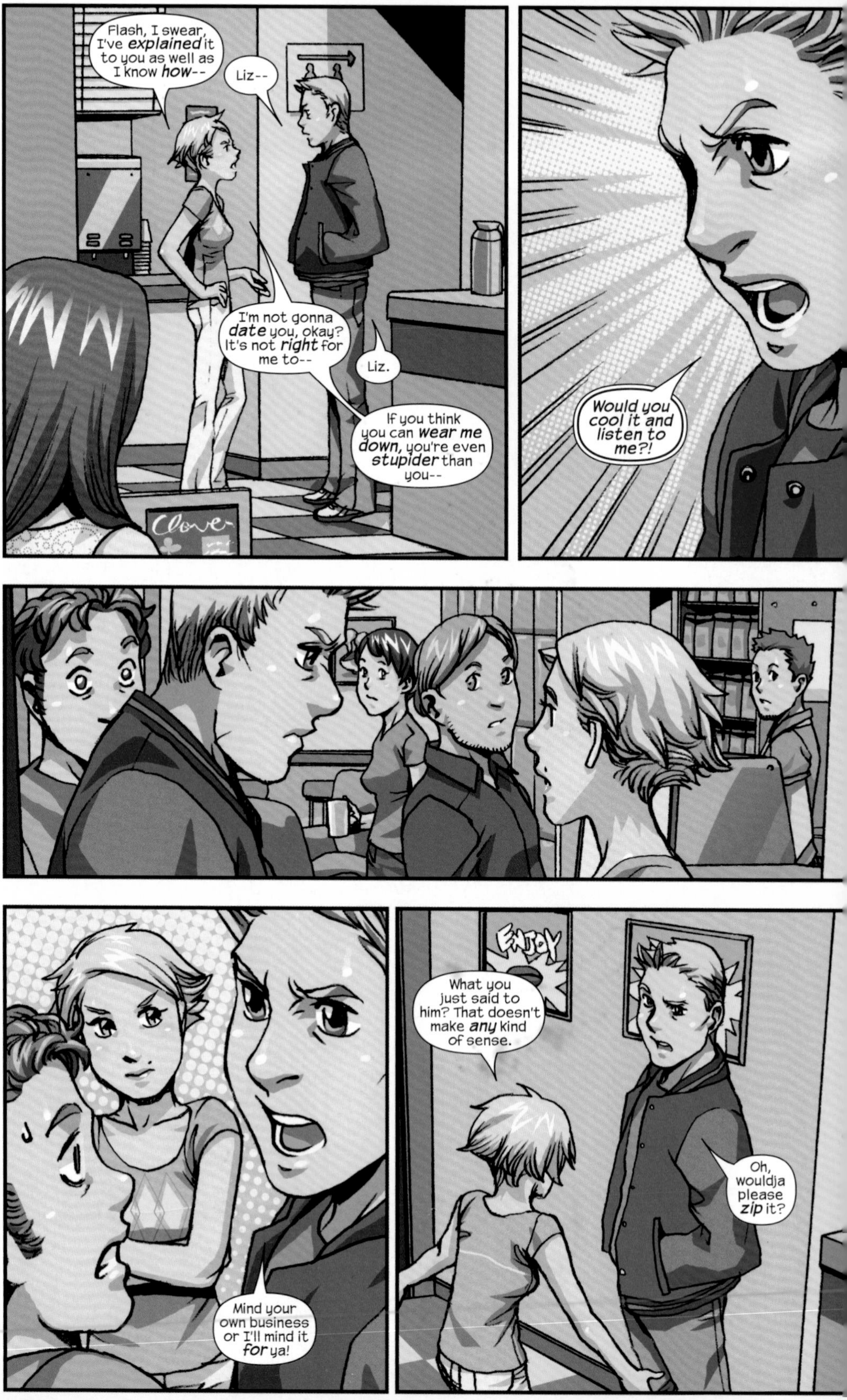
Flash, I swear, I've *explained* it to you as well as I know *how*--
Liz--
I'm not gonna *date* you, okay? It's not *right* for me to--
Liz.
If you think you can **wear me down,** you're even *stupider* than you--
Would you cool it and listen to me?!
What you just said to him? That doesn't make *any* kind of sense.
Oh, wouldja please *zip* it?
Mind your own business or I'll mind it *for* ya!

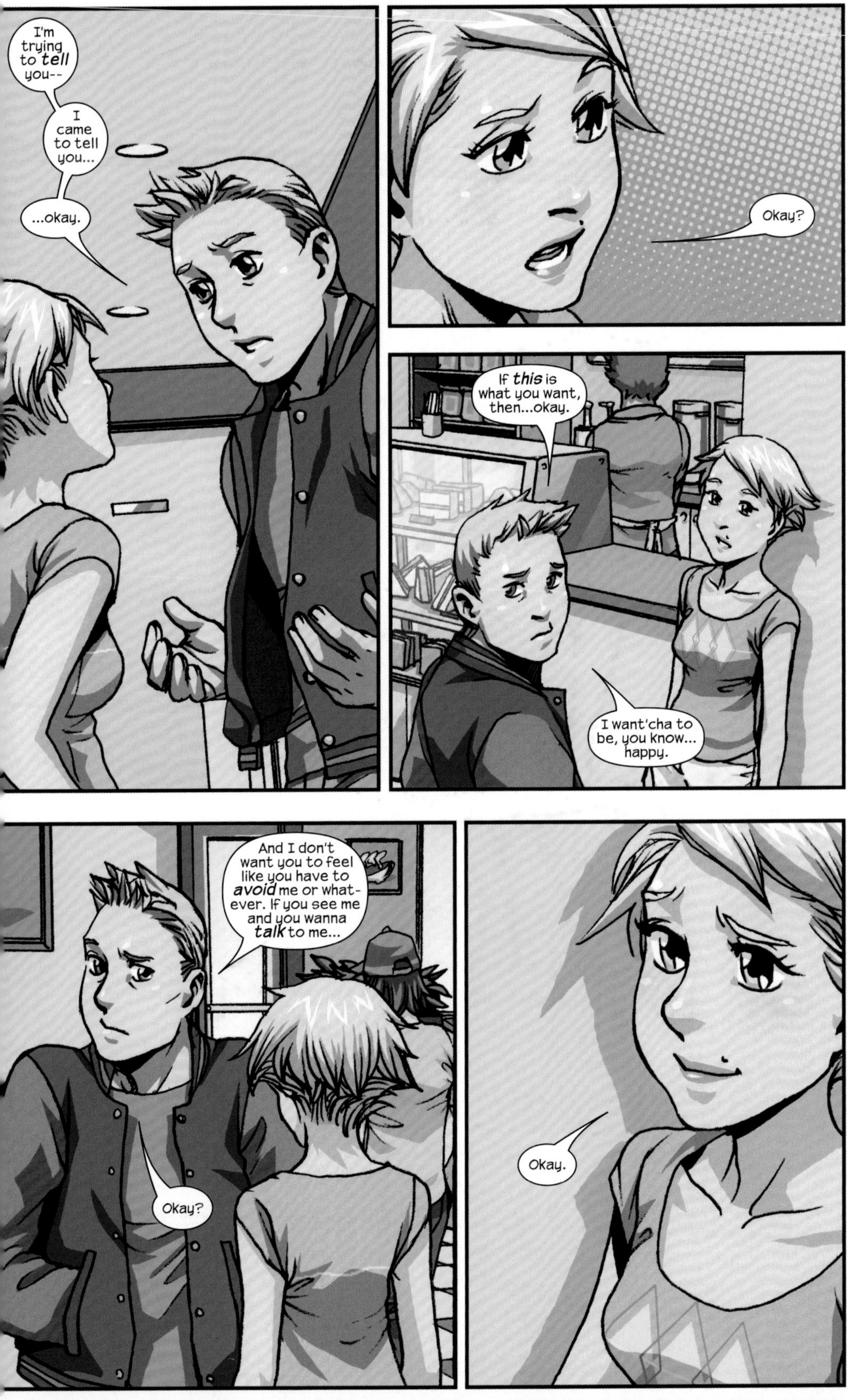
I'm trying to tell you--
I came to tell you...
...okay.
Okay?
If this is what you want, then...okay.
I want'cha to be, you know... happy.
And I don't want you to feel like you have to avoid me or what-ever. If you see me and you wanna talk to me...
Okay?
Okay.

Liz... what was *that*?

I dunno how, but I think Flash finally got an ounce of *common sense.*

Are you *crying?*

Shut it, Watson.

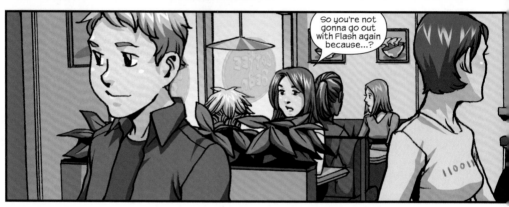

So you're not gonna go out with Flash again because...?

Because I realized I missed having a *boyfriend* more than I missed Flash.

Because dating just to be dating isn't a good enough reason.

And, hey...

...being single is *hardly* the end of the world, right?

Besides-- it *does* have its share of *benefits*.

Yeah? Like what?

Duh.

THE SINGLE THING

Spider-Man Loves Mary Jane #9

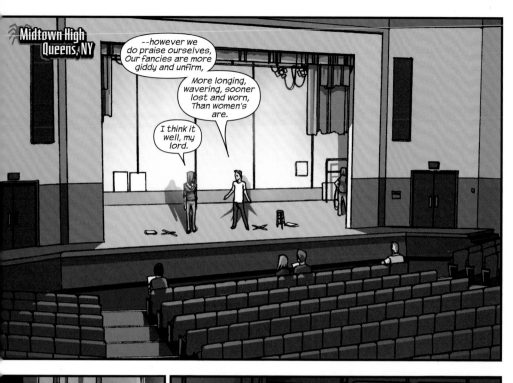

--however we do praise ourselves, Our fancies are more giddy and unfirm,

More longing, wavering, sooner lost and worn, Than women's are.

I think it well, my lord.

Then let thy love be younger than thyself, Or thy affection cannot hold the bent;

For women are as roses, whose fair flower Being once display'd, doth fall that very hour.

Excuse me, young lady...

Your line, MJ.

Hello...? Anybody home?

I say how fickle *guys* are when it comes to women, and then you *agree* with me.

That's how the scene *works*, remember?

Bye, MJ.

Yeah. Bye.

You were pretty *good* in there.

Oh. Thanks, Gwen.

I mean, what I *saw* of it.

Yeah. *Mr. Tiplady* doesn't like what he calls--

--"interlopers." Yeah, that cracked me up.

Who *uses* words like that?

Bad sci-fi villains?

Heh, yeah...

Oh. Um...

Peter and I were gonna hang out, but he suddenly remembered he had to help his *aunt* with something?

So he asked me to tell you he couldn't meet you for *algebra* tonight.

Oh. Okay.

Well, I guess I'll--

Mary Jane, wait!

Heh, sorry. I figured...since, well, Peter and I are becoming *friends* and stuff...

...and since the two of *you* are friends, and neither of us are *up* to anything now...

You wanna go get a *burger* or something?

--was the scene *mere minutes ago* as *Spider-Man* took on the mysterious *Looter* once again on *and* over the streets of Queens--their *fifth* known confrontation in the past two weeks.

While the webbed crime fighter appeared to be at the *top* of his *game,* the Looter slipped away yet again--*this* time after robbing a *local* jewelry store...

Wow, that wasn't far from here.

Are you a Spidey fan?

A *fan?*

The guy *puts* on a disguise, runs around on his *own authority* and gets in the way of *real* police work.

Well, that's what my *dad* says, anyway. And I kinda see his point, I guess.

Actually, that's why I was *watching*--to see if my dad was there.

He's a cop?

A *captain,* yeah. He's why I'm here.

In Queens, I mean.

He used to work in the *city* but got *transferred* or whatever...

...and he has this whole thing about, "I *have* to live in the *community* I'm paid to *protect* and serve," so...

Does that happen *a lot*?

Oh, only every few years...it's like, just as soon as I feel comfy where I'm *at*, it's time to pack up.

That's why *Peter's* been so *great*.

Yeah, he's--

What do you mean, exactly?

I'm not really the *greatest* at making new friends.

You know that *filter* everyone has that stops them from saying stupid things? I don't really *have* that.

But you haven't--

I've been trying to control it. But when I'm with *Peter*...

...I don't really *have* to. He's just so understanding.

He's... *genuine*.

Durr. What am I saying?

You know *exactly* what I'm talking about. You've known Peter *way* longer than me...

Yeah...

BEAUTY FULL

He really *likes* you, you know.

He talks about you *all the time.*

Like, he'll comment on something and then he'll relate it to something you *did* or something you *said...*

Urrgh.

See, *this* is what I'm talking about. No filter.

I totally shouldn't have told you that.

But... yeah.

He likes you.

Mary Jane, do you know what this *means*?

He's all *yours!*

I don't see how you figure--

Gwen *told* you Peter likes you. Why would she tell you that if she wanted him for herself?

Weren't you *listening*? She doesn't think before she speaks, sometimes. It slipped out. She didn't *mean* to tell me.

And if Gwen *did* mean to, it's *probably* because she wants so badly to make new friends that she felt uncomfortable and used that as an *icebreaker.*

Gee, MJ-- don't you think you could come up with an excuse that's just a *little* more *contrived?*

"Contrived?"

I learned a word. Don't make me hurt you.

Look, you're obviously scared of telling Peter how you *feel* and stuff, but--

This isn't *about* that, Liz. I mean...I could *see* it.

The way she looked when she talked about him...

Okay, so she's into him. So what?

If you like Peter as much as I *think* you do, you should stand your ground. *And* you should come up with a *battle plan.*

A battle plan. Really.

Now that you're her friend, you can *use* that to your *advantage.* You can find her *weaknesses.*

I could never--

I *guarantee* you she's doing the same thing.

See, that's the thing, Liz...

...I guarantee you she *isn't.* Gwen's a nice person.

Oh, geez...

The Home-coming Queen and the pretty new *blonde* chick are after the same *nerd.*

What's *wrong* with this world?

Mary Jane. *There* you are.

Trish. Hey.

Harry said you were cool with us *dating*, so I hope this isn't too, you know...

You hope what isn't too *what*?

It's just, I was kinda wondering...

...maybe you've noticed...

...do you think Harry's been acting *strange* lately?

I don't *believe* this!

You girls aren't conspiring *against* me, are you?

Believe it or not, Harry, not *everything's* about *you.*

Pff. *Prove* it.

So...what **are** we talking about?

Uh...

Um...

Heya, Mary J--

Gwen! Awesome! Hi!

Gwen, is it? Harry Osborn.

I'd been meaning to introduce myself for a **while** now.

O-okay...

Excuse us. I think it's time to go...

What're you--?

Time. To. **Go**.

Wow. He's not **at all** subtle, is he?

He used to be. For a **little** while, anyway...

Well... you *know*, if you wanted me to, I could maybe...

Well, I guess when you're as *cute* as he is, you can get *away* with the jack-hammer approach...

You think he's cute?

Oh, come on. He's *gorgeous*.

Mary Jane? You could what?

Mm? Oh. Nothing.

Just... nothing.

Okay...

Anyway, Harry's not my *type*.

I'll take a guy who can make me laugh over a stud muffin *any* day.

Know what I mean?

May I be
excused?

What am
I supposed
to do?

Did I just catch you *talking to yourself?*

HH!

Peter!

Didn't mean to startle you. How've you *been,* stranger?

How've *you* been?

I can't complain. You know.

Yeah...

So...I guess one of these days we should actually *keep* our *study appointments,* huh?

Yeah, I'm sorry about that.

It's mostly me. I've just been... so *busy,* you know?

Yeah. Yeah, me too.

I've been... doing lots of stuff and...

...stuff.

How's Harry?

Harry... he's, uh...

Why are you asking me about Harry? Don't you guys *talk* anymore?

Uh--

Well, yeah. Yeah. I guess, uh...

I guess I was just trying to make *conversation*...

You crack me up, Peter Parker.

Yeah.

Well, hey, uh...Gwen and I were gonna go to the *arcade* for a little bit later on tonight, and we thought...

...maybe you'd like to *come along*?

Thank you, Peter.

But no, I... I'm usually too *exhausted* after rehearsal to go out or any-thing.

Sure. No, that's cool. I totally understand.

I better get this to the lab.

Yeah.

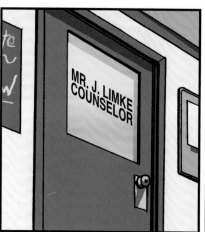

MR. J. LIMKE
COUNSELOR

I, um...

There's someone I like. I mean, someone I *care* about?

And I *wanna* tell him, it's just...

There's this *girl* he's hanging out with...and I'm pretty sure *she* likes him, too.

They're not dating.

Maybe they'd wind up making a perfect couple. If I got in the *way* of that--

Maybe *you* and this someone would make the perfect couple. Have you considered that?

Hhh...

She's really *nice*, you know? And she doesn't have a lot of friends.

I wouldn't want to, like, *hurt* her or whatever...

Okay. So what do you think is the *real* reason you can't tell him how you feel?

I'm *not* lying. That's how I *feel.*

Those aren't feelings, Miss Watson.

They're *excuses.*

I want you to do something for me. I want you to *think* about the possibility of telling him.

How does *that* make you feel?

Afraid?

I feel afraid.

Good. That's very good.

I'm going to *tell* you something, Miss Watson. Something very important. Something you should never forget.

You only get *one shot* at life.

You can spend it almost *entirely* without risk, no question. Practically *everybody* does it.

But the thing you need to *understand* is--

--without risk, *there is no reward.*

If happiness is within your grasp, you *need* to take that chance.

You need to reach out and *take* it!

Are you with me?

...so I told Liana that she *can't* just make up whatever old cheer she wants just *'cause*, you know?

I mean, there's a *pecking order!*

I'm in charge. *I* decide. Me. Liz Allen.

Plus, there's no *way* I'm going to wear a cheese head--

MJ?

MJ, it's the bus. We're goin' over to *my place*, remember?

You comin'?

No.

I'm not.

I'm going to the arcade.

Go get him, girl.

⸮heff...⸮

⸮...hnn...⸮

⸮...henh...⸮

GAAAAH!

No no no no!

It's almost over for you...

HA!

Yes! I beat you!

I *beat* you! In your *face*, Parker!

Man! And I was so close, too...

Waitaminute... you *let* me win, didn't you?

PFF. You don't know what you're talking about.

You *did* let me win.

Tch. So sweet...

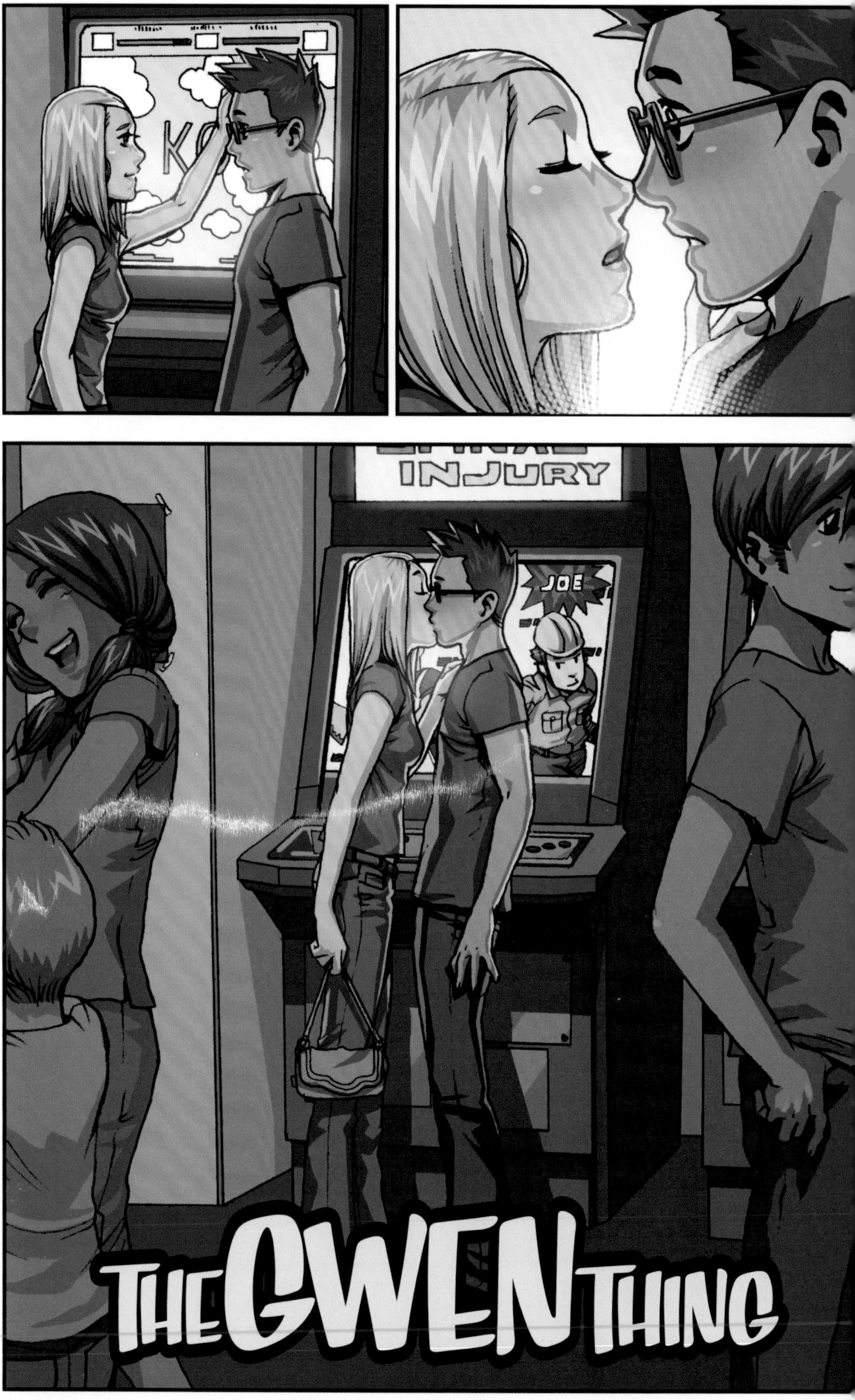
KO
INJURY
JOE
THE GWEN THING

Spider-Man Loves Mary Jane #10

We're not tellin' him. We *can't.*

We *can't* not tell him.

When it goes down, he'll *know* it was us. Is he gonna have our *backs* or will he think we *dissed* him?

Yeah, well, he can't *rat us out* if he doesn't know anything, can he?

But Flash is *one* of us, man. We *owe* it to him to at least *tell* him.

Tell me what?

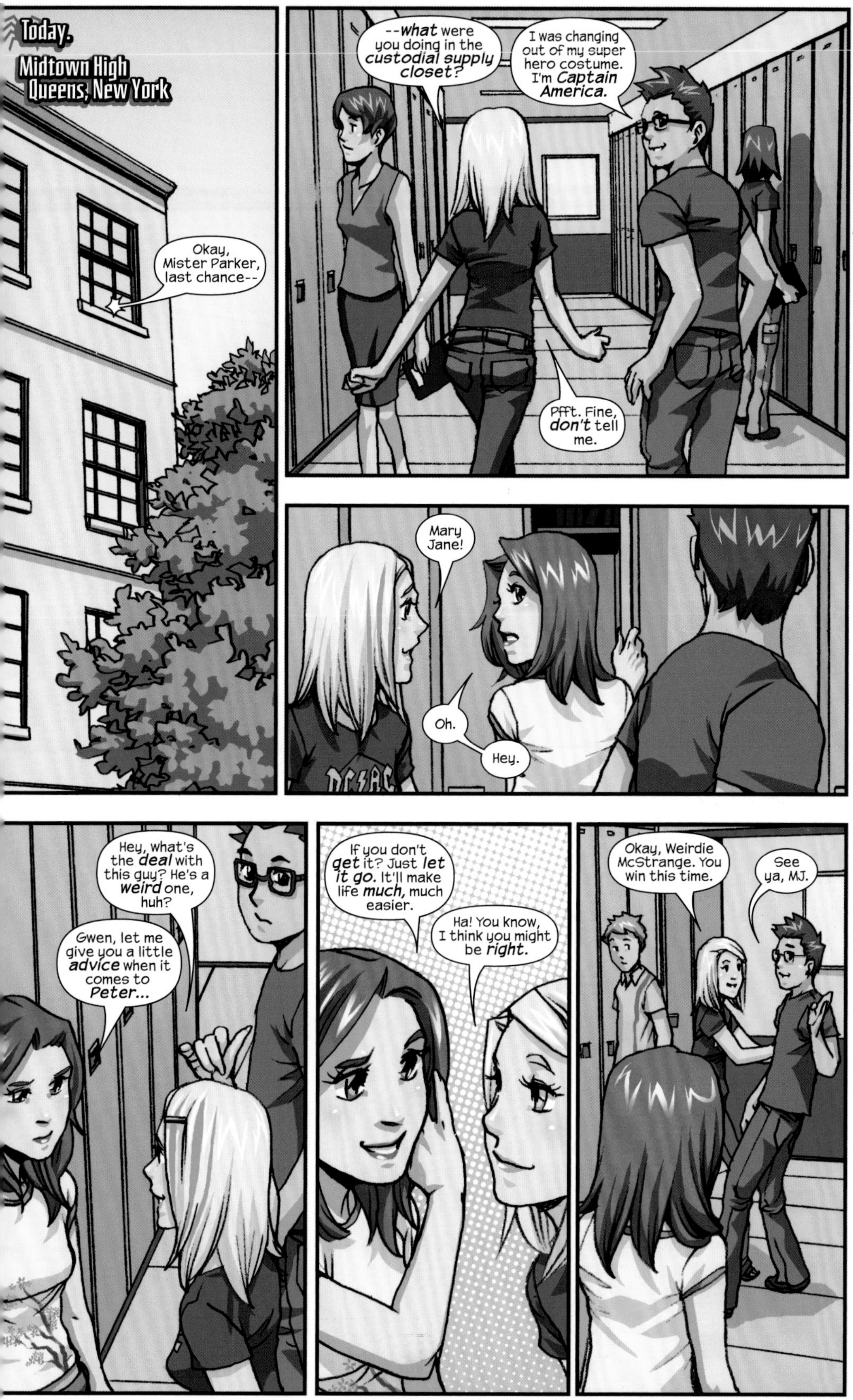
Today.
Midtown High
Queens, New York
Okay, Mister Parker, last chance--
--what were you doing in the custodial supply closet?
I was changing out of my super hero costume. I'm Captain America.
Pfft. Fine, don't tell me.
Mary Jane!
Oh.
Hey.
Hey, what's the deal with this guy? He's a weird one, huh?
Gwen, let me give you a little advice when it comes to Peter...
If you don't get it? Just let it go. It'll make life much, much easier.
Ha! You know, I think you might be right.
Okay, Weirdie McStrange. You win this time.
See ya, MJ.

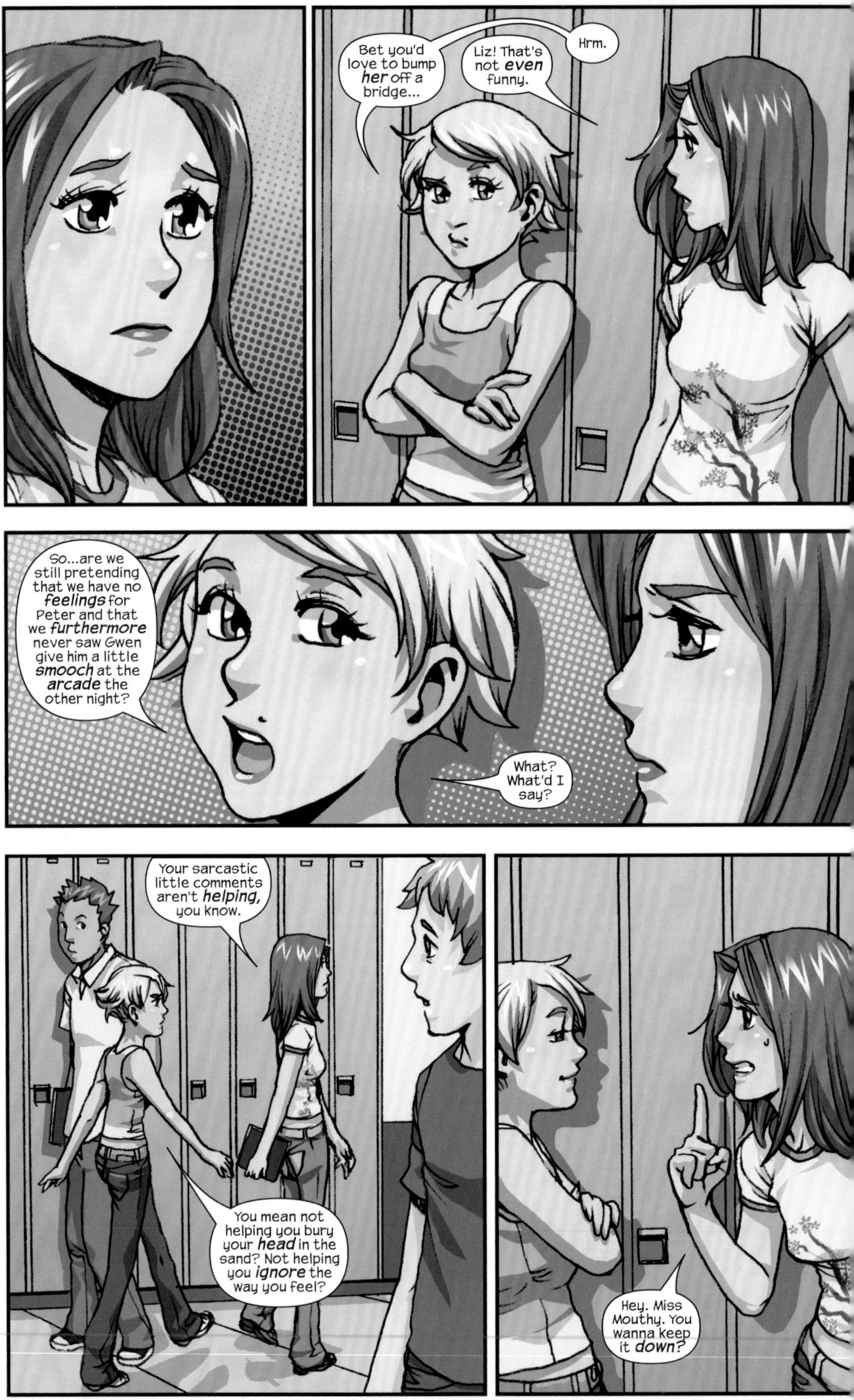
Bet you'd love to bump *her* off a bridge...
Liz! That's not *even* funny.
Hrm.
So...are we still pretending that we have no *feelings* for Peter and that we *furthermore* never saw Gwen give him a little *smooch* at the *arcade* the other night?
What? What'd I say?
Your sarcastic little comments aren't *helping,* you know.
You mean not helping you bury your *head* in the sand? Not helping you *ignore* the way you feel?
Hey. Miss Mouthy. You wanna keep it *down?*

Anyway, what am I supposed to do? They're *obviously* a couple now.

Really? They are? Then how come I never see them even *holding hands*?

Peter and Gwen don't look any more like a *couple* than Peter and *you* did.

Well, hey, look-- I can't meet you at the *Bean* tonight. And *you* can't go there, either.

What? Why not?

Flash wants to talk to me there after practice, and he said he doesn't even want to *see* you there.

Are you *kidding* me? He still *hates* me *that much*?

Geez...

So... what does he *want*?

Flash...

...are you gonna tell me what you want or am I gonna **break** **your face?**

Would you cut that stuff out? This ain't exactly **easy** for me, you know.

The play. MJ's play? It opens on a Friday. Same time as--

Yeah, same night as your next game. So?

Our next game is a **huge** game, Liz.

The guys... they're kinda takin' it **personal.** Like the **drama** people did it **on purpose,** you know? So they, uh...

They wanna trash the stage.

THEY WHAT?!

Flash Thompson--

Hey, would you keep it **down?** Geez, you're like a **fire alarm!**

Look, it's not like I *want* 'em to, all right? It's their idea.

But they're my *teammates*, Liz. There's no *way* I can *rat* on 'em. And they'd *know* it was me, too. They didn't even wanna *tell* me about it 'cause of--

You know, with MJ.

Gahh...

I dunno what to do.

Flash. You gigantic, ridiculous *dope.*

Don't you know? They all *look up* to you. You're their leader.

So *lead* them.

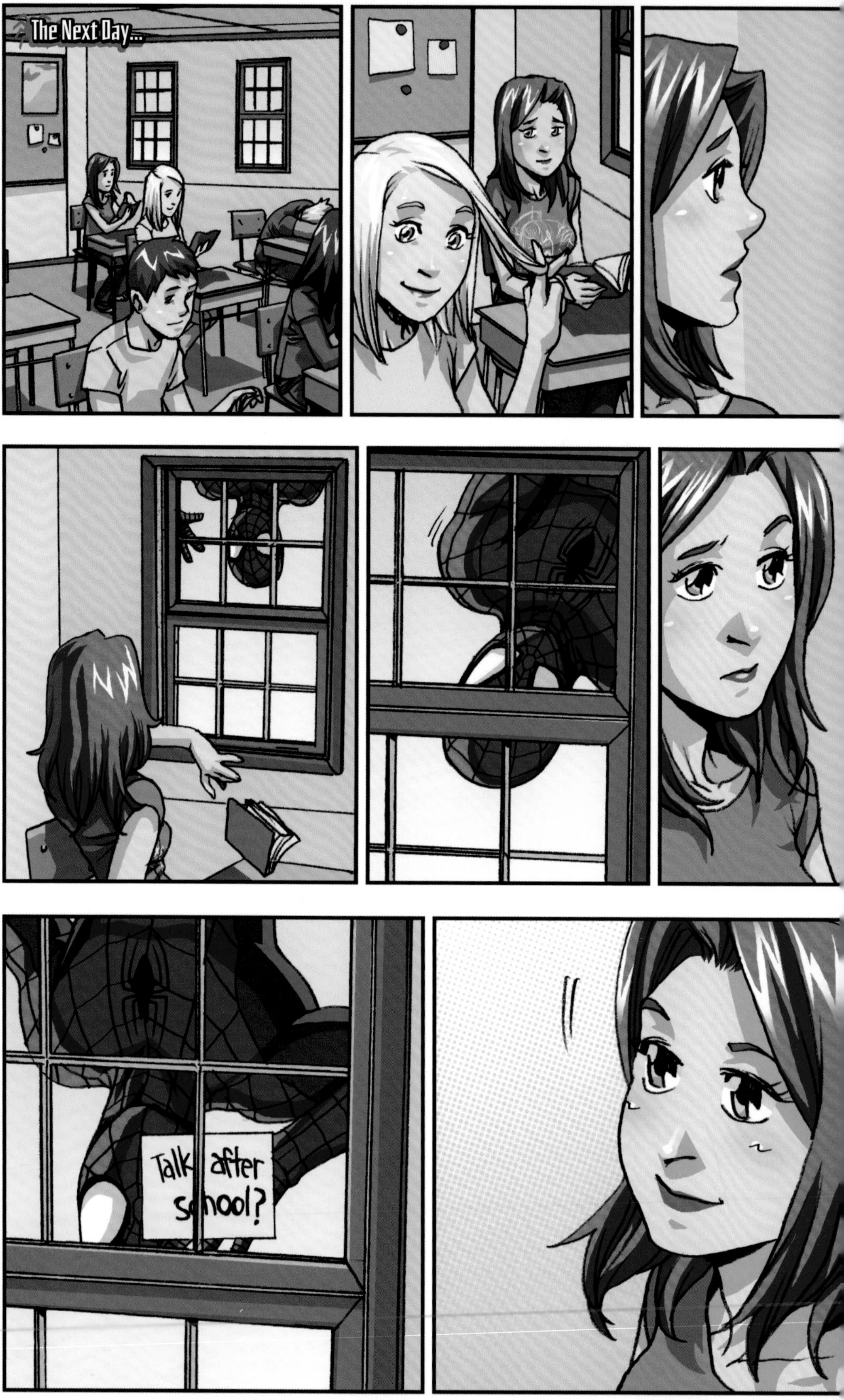
The Next Day...
Talk after school?

It's so *nice* up here.

It's like... taking a step back from the whole *world*, you know?

Heh...like I'm telling *you* anything new...

So, how's your little *hunt* going?

I'm telling you, MJ...it's driving me *nuts*.

I just can't get a *handle* on this *Looter* guy!

I *know* he's come here right after a few of his robberies, so I figure he's *at least* gotta have a stash of *stolen goods* around here somewhere...!

If I could just *catch* him one of these times...

You'll get him, Spidey. Of *course* you will.

Sometimes it just takes *time*, right?

Good practice, guys! *Great* practice!

Got that right! We're *definitely* gonna be kickin' butt next week.

You mean the *game*, or, uh... the *other* thing?

Hey, the *other* thing's a piece of *cake*. Just gotta make sure none of the *drama snobs* are around when we get *into* it.

Ain't that right, Flash?

Hey, ya know, I was thinkin' about all that, and...I think I got a *better* idea.

Really.

Yeah! We, uh... we *promote* the play.

No, seriously. See, uh...if we respond to their scheduling with *kindness?* Then... *we're* the bigger people.

Dude, we're *already* bigger. Why d'you think we're on the *football team?*

No, man, what I *mean* is--

Actually, what I *really* mean is...

...we're not *doin'* it. We're not trashing the stage.

What, 'cause *you* say so?

Yeah, 'cause I say so! And 'cause it's *wrong!*

You guys all *know* ruining the play is wrong. Why ya wanna do it? 'Cause the drama people *dis-respected* us?

Did they do it on purpose? Doubt it. It's *possible*, though, so I'll give you that, but...

But SO WHAT?!

We *all know* that 98 percent of the people *goin'* to that stupid show on opening night-- they weren't gonna go to our game *anyway!*

Tell me I'm wrong.

Heh heh!

Something *funny?*

Mary Jane Watson turned you down in front of the *entire school*, man...

...so *why* are you still so *whipped?*

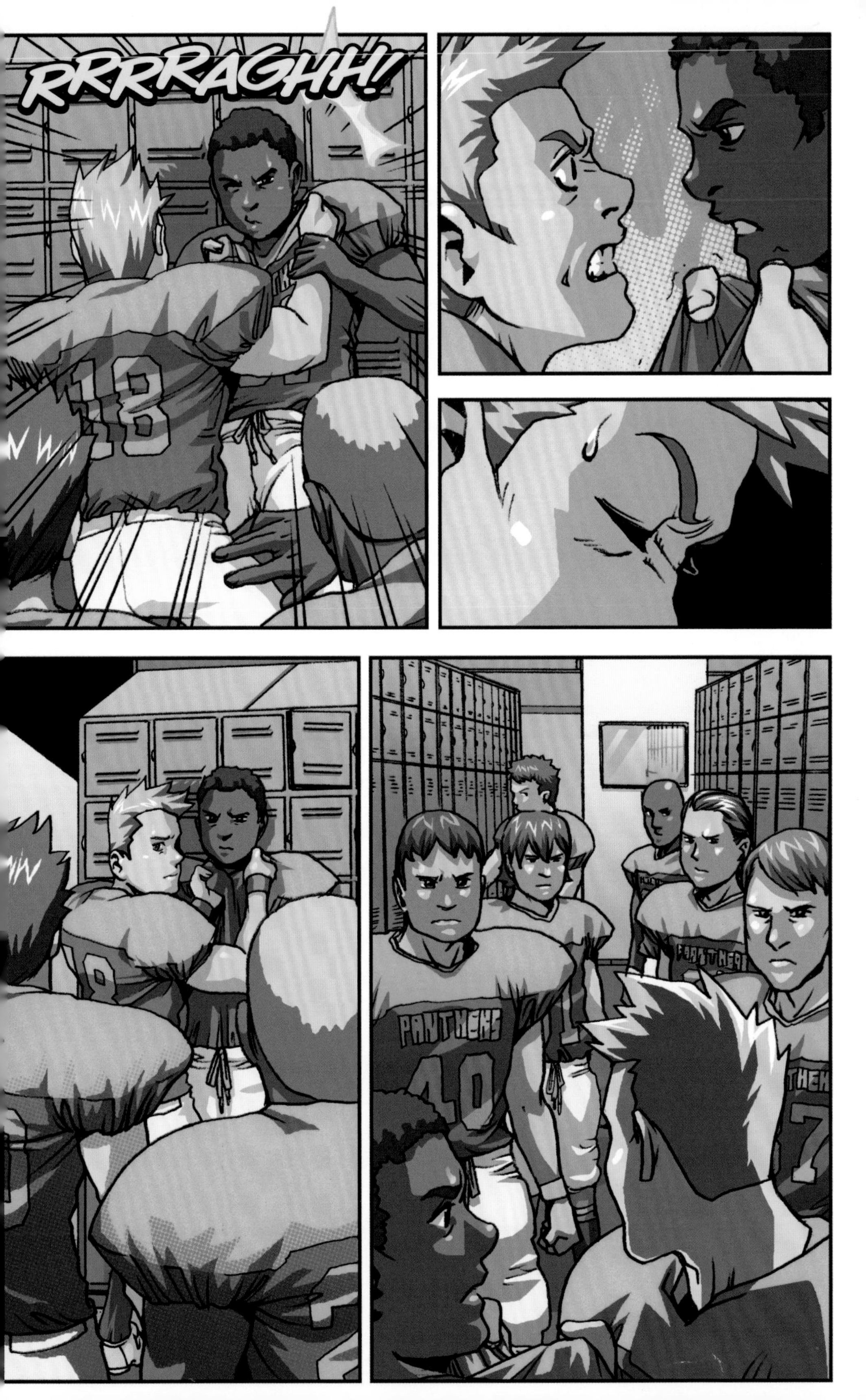
RRRRAGHH!
PANTHERS

Hey, Utah.

Y-yeah...?

You just got promoted.

Quarterback. First string.

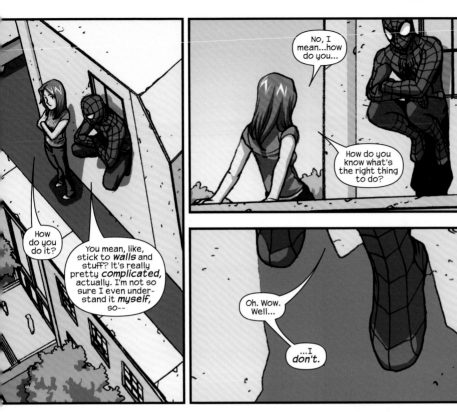

No, I mean...how do you...

How do you know what's the right thing to do?

How do you do it?

You mean, like, stick to *walls* and stuff? It's really pretty *complicated*, actually. I'm not so sure I even understand it *myself*, so--

Oh. Wow. Well...

...I *don't*.

I struggle with it *every day*.

Growing up, I was taught... you know, you're told to *behave* a certain way, and you're given these *morals* to live by. You're *told* what's right and what's wrong, but it's...

It's all kinda *vague*, isn't it?

Yeah. Yeah, it's all black and white with *maybe* some gray sprinkled in... but we live in a *Roy G. Biv* world. So, you just listen to what you've learned, you listen to your *gut*, you hold your breath...

...and then you take the *plunge*.

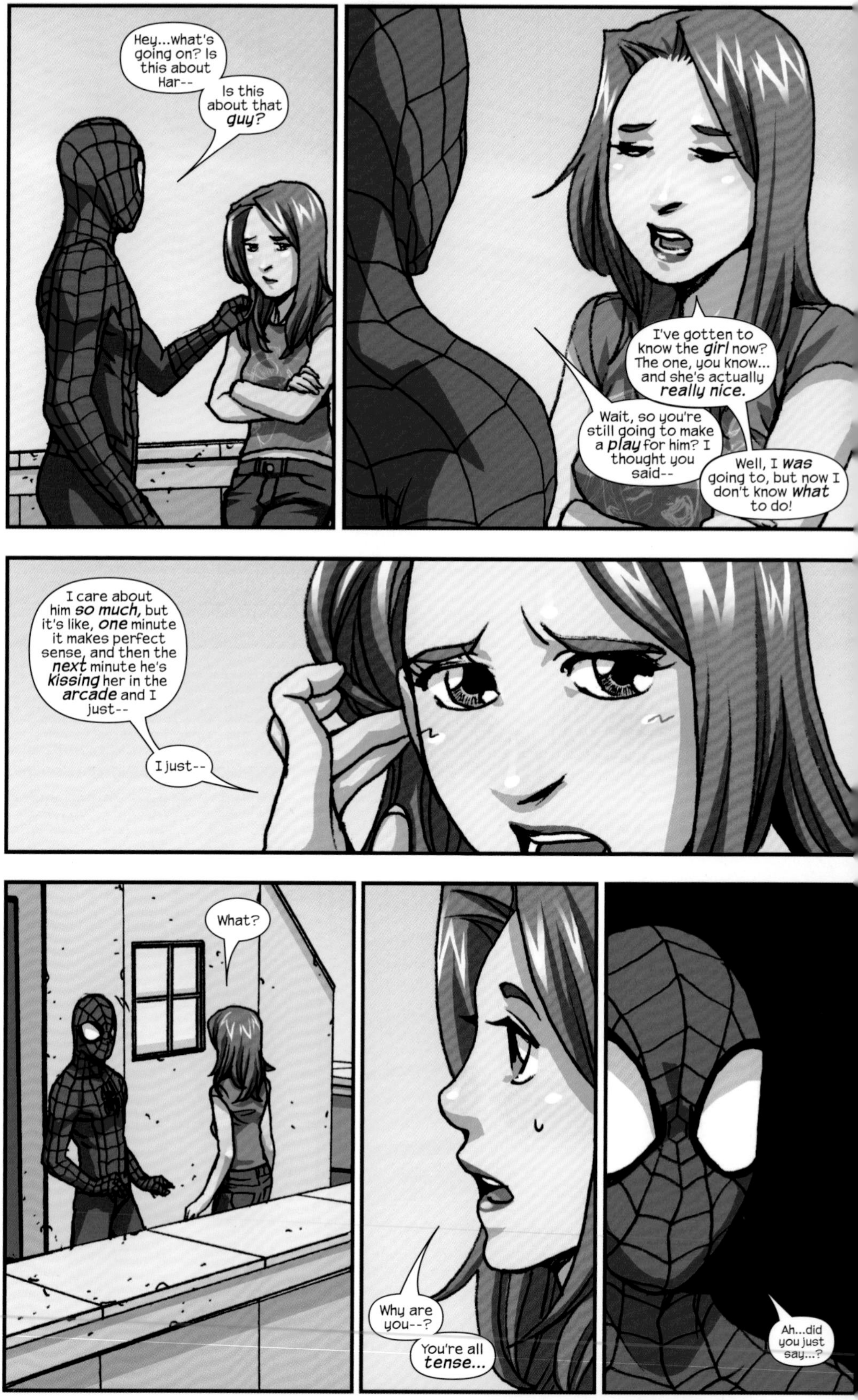
Hey...what's going on? Is this about Har--
Is this about that *guy?*
I've gotten to know the *girl* now? The one, you know... and she's actually ***really nice.***
Wait, so you're still going to make a *play* for him? I thought you said--
Well, I *was* going to, but now I don't know *what* to do!
I care about him *so much,* but it's like, *one* minute it makes perfect sense, and then the *next* minute he's *kissing* her in the *arcade* and I just--
I just--
What?
Why are you--?
You're all *tense...*
Ah...did you just say...?

HHHhh!

Nice try, *Looter*--

--but didn't you know you can't sneak up on a spider?

AAAAAA!

Ah-*ah*, Purple Pants--

--the fight's *over* here!

Confident as *ever*, I see...

...but I'm sure I *explained* this to you already!

I'm *faster* than you!

I'm *stronger* than you!

And I'm *sick* of you trying to *hunt me down!*

Ohmygosh!

You.

What are you *doing* up here? You shouldn't be--

HEY!

You don't come *near* her!

I've had *enough* of you, "Looter"...

What are you--?

...so let's just meet the guy *behind* the mask!

Huh.

MR. LIMKE!

Miss Watson, I--

I--

I don't... I don't **understand.** You, of all people...?

Wearing a mask...it made everything so much **easier**...

I could do anything I wanted without...without **consequence.**

Miss Watson. Mary Jane.

I'm so ashamed.

And I am **sorry.**

There was a meteorite exhibit... one of the rocks, it... it *called* to me...it *gave* me this *power*...

Why me... why *me*?

Yeah, I hear ya, bud.

I've gotta get him to the cops. But, MJ, I think we really, um...

Yeah?

Nothing. It's, uh...it's nothing.

If happiness is within your grasp, you *need* to take that chance.

Who could it *be* this late?

Don't worry, Aunt May. I've got--

--it.

Hey, Peter.

Hey.

I know it's late, and I know I could have *called*, but...

...I have something to *tell* you, and it's *important*, and I *have* to do it *now*.

So...I guess I'll just come out and say it.

Peter...

THE RIGHT THING

Spider-Man Loves Mary Jane #11

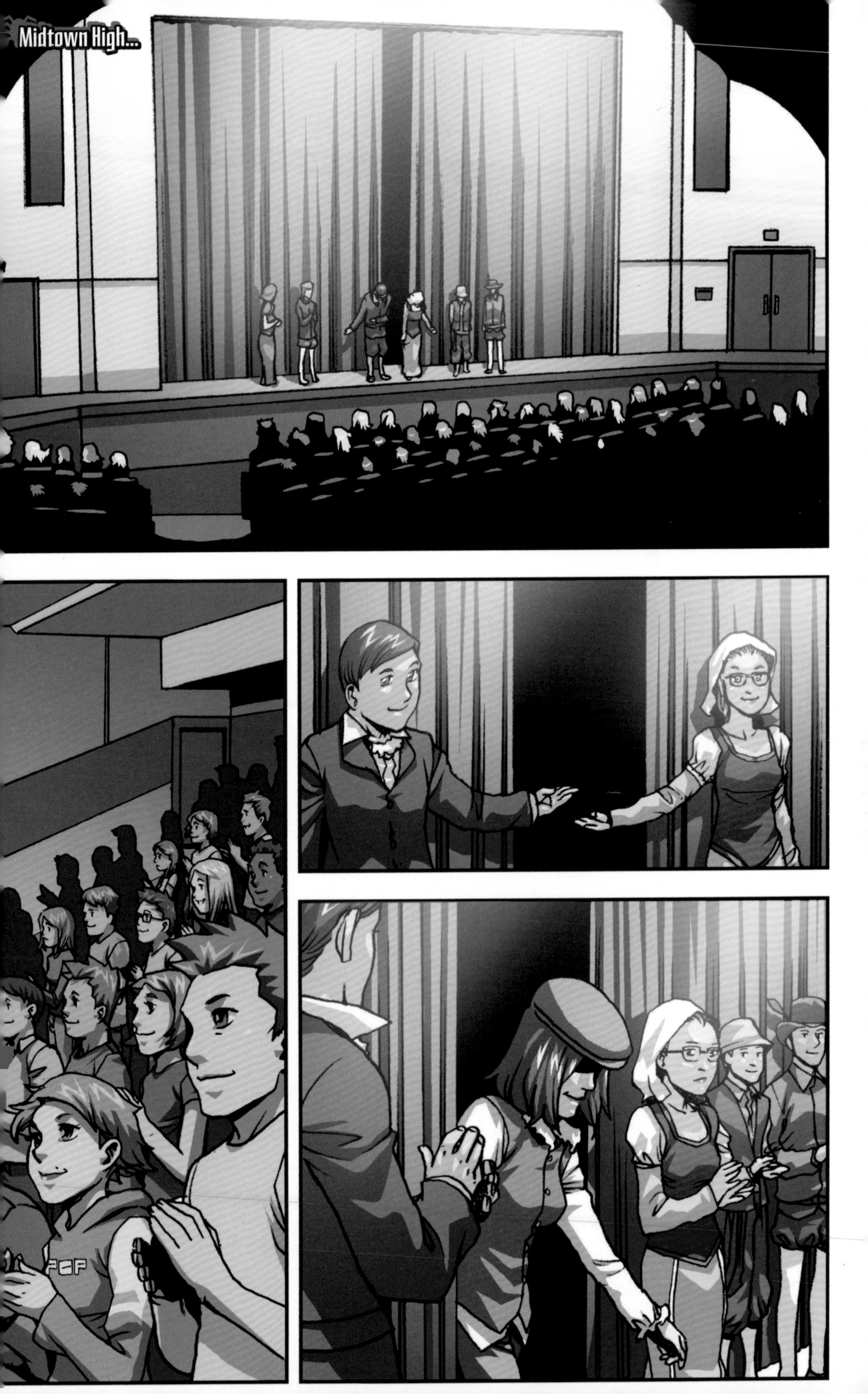
Midtown High...
POP

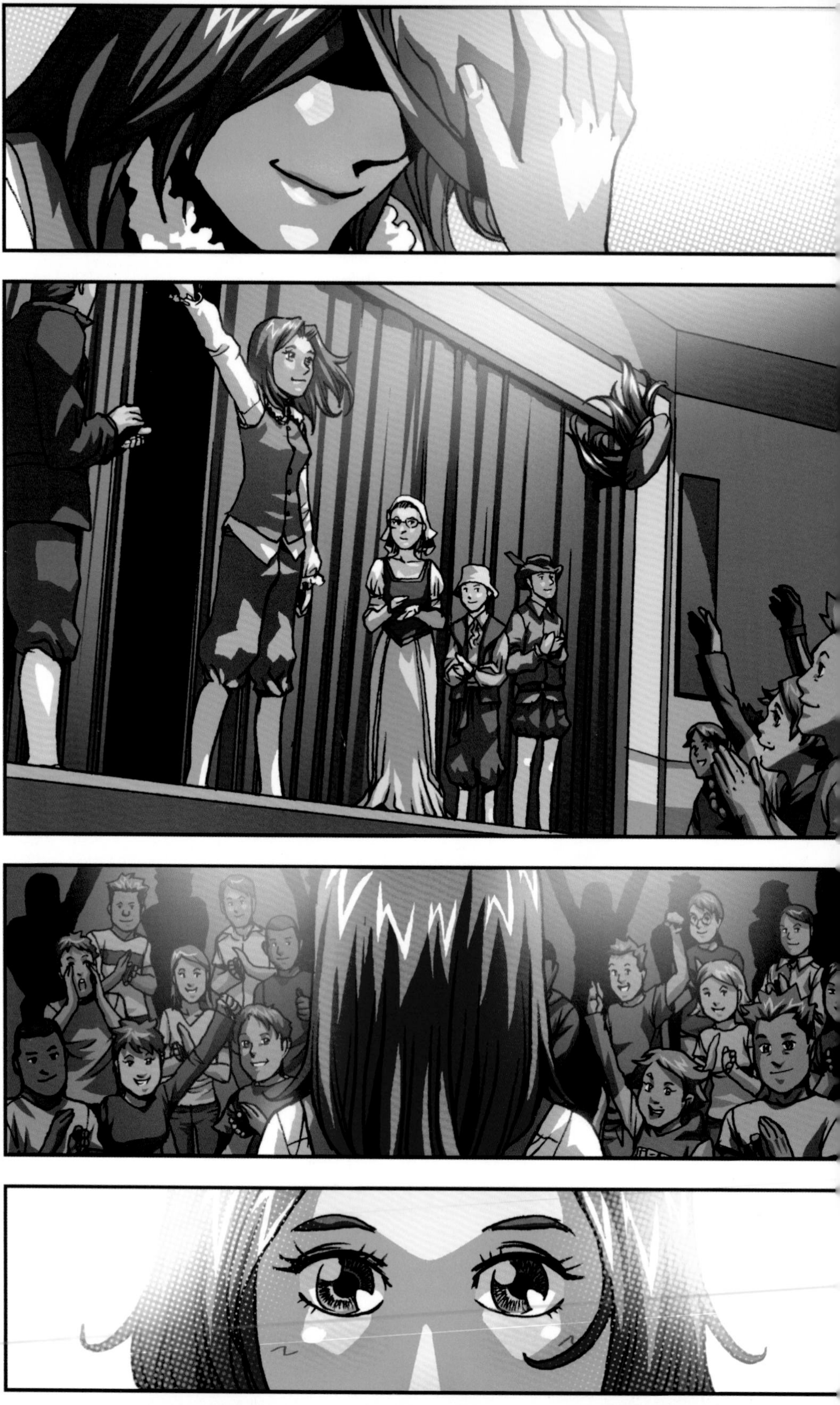

TWELFTH NIGHT

FINAL DAY!!!

I didn't understand a word of it, but I'll *tell* ya...

...seein' MJ as a *guy*? That demolished every last bit of interest I ever *had* in her.

Awesome. You being in love with MJ is *exactly* what I wanted to be reminded of. *So* romantic.

Stop it, would ya? I only mentioned it so you'd know I don't *think* of her as--

That I don't--

You *know* what I mean, okay? I ain't gonna say it.

Heh!

Now I'm *really* glad you and the rest of the football team didn't *trash* their set.

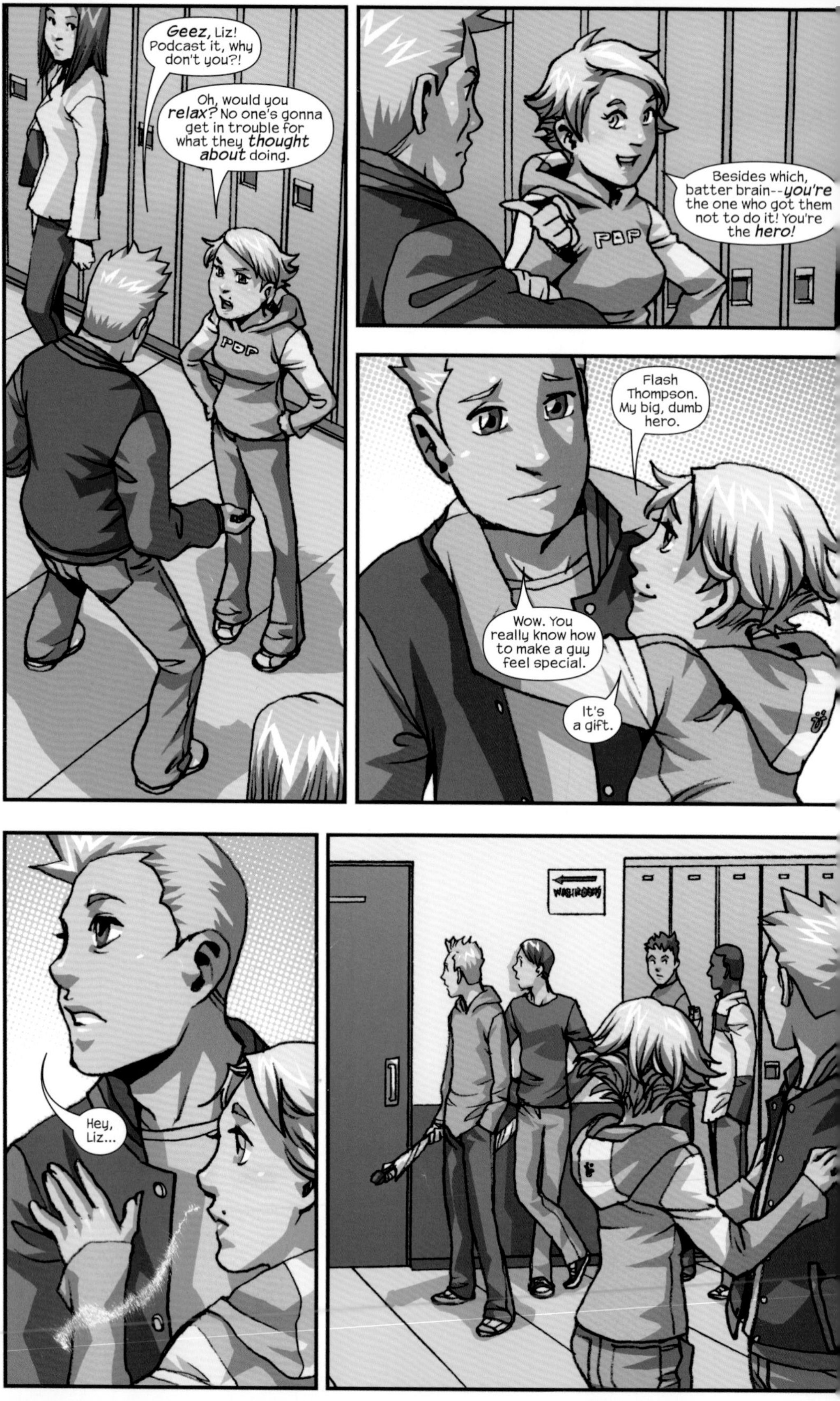
Geez, Liz! Podcast it, why don't you?!
Oh, would you relax? No one's gonna get in trouble for what they thought about doing.
Besides which, batter brain--you're the one who got them not to do it! You're the hero!
Flash Thompson. My big, dumb hero.
Wow. You really know how to make a guy feel special.
It's a gift.
Hey, Liz...

Liz!

Flash!

I'm so glad you guys came!

Oh, whatever. You *know* I wouldn't miss your acting debut.

I would've seen it *earlier,* of course, but I had to convince the *caveman* here to come along.

Wow, a rose! I bet I know who *that's* from...!

Well, then you know more than I do. I've got a couple *dozen* back there, each from a different "secret admirer."

Heh!

I can't tell if you're joking.

Excuse me...Mary Jane?

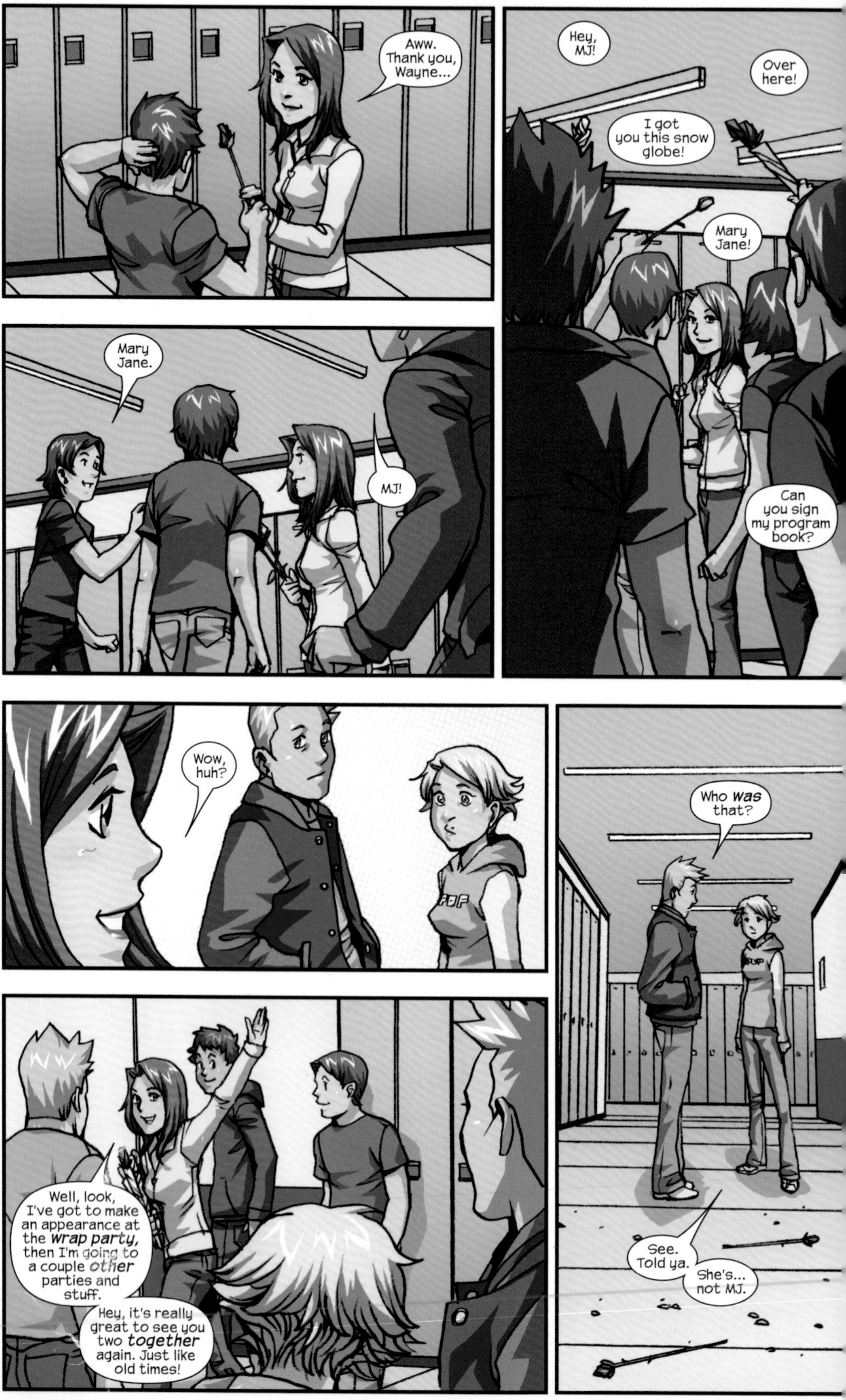
Aww. Thank you, Wayne...
Hey, MJ!
Over here!
I got you this snow globe!
Mary Jane!
Can you sign my program book?
Mary Jane.
MJ!
Wow, huh?
Well, look, I've got to make an appearance at the *wrap party,* then I'm going to a couple *other* parties and stuff.
Hey, it's really great to see you two *together* again. Just like old times!
Who *was* that?
See. Told ya.
She's... not MJ.

I don't know what it is you want me to tell you.

What I--?

Why?! I *want* you to tell me *why*.

It's not what you think--

Oh, what-*ever!*

You were *kissing* her, Harry. There is absolutely *no way* it's anything *but* a desecration of our relationship.

No. You're missing the point, Trish.

You and me--our "relationship"?

It was never all that. It was just...fun.

Norah, hey.

I just ended it with Trish. We're cool, right?

ONE LOVE

No, Harry, we're *not* cool. I thought it already *was* over between you.

Hey, I never said that...

No, but you never said you *were* still dating her when I *asked* you about it, either!

OPEN

Such a jerk!

Go through a lotta girls.

What?

I *said*, you *seem* to go through a lot of *girls*.

I guess. But, you know, I'll take a good time over a girlfriend *any* day.

Yeah, I hear *that...*

Still, after a while it *gets* to a guy, know what I mean? You start to want...something *more*.

I don't know you, do I?

Name's *Luke.*

Harry.

I have *two rules,* Luke--never let yourself get too *attached,* and always keep an eye out for the *next* one.

And that works for you?

Like a charm. No regrets.

Okay, then... who's *next* for you?

Right there. Liana. She's a cheerleader.

What about you? You got one picked out?

Nice.

Yeah, I do. Right over there.

Redhead.

Pick someone else, dude.

What? No way, man. She's *fine.*

Dude...I am *not* gonna say it *again.*

Heh heh heh!

Sounds like *Harry* don't follow his *rules* too well!

Yeah. Okay.

Aww, you guys are too swe--

MJ.

Harry!

Harry, you know Matt and Caleb, right?

Hey. 'Sup.

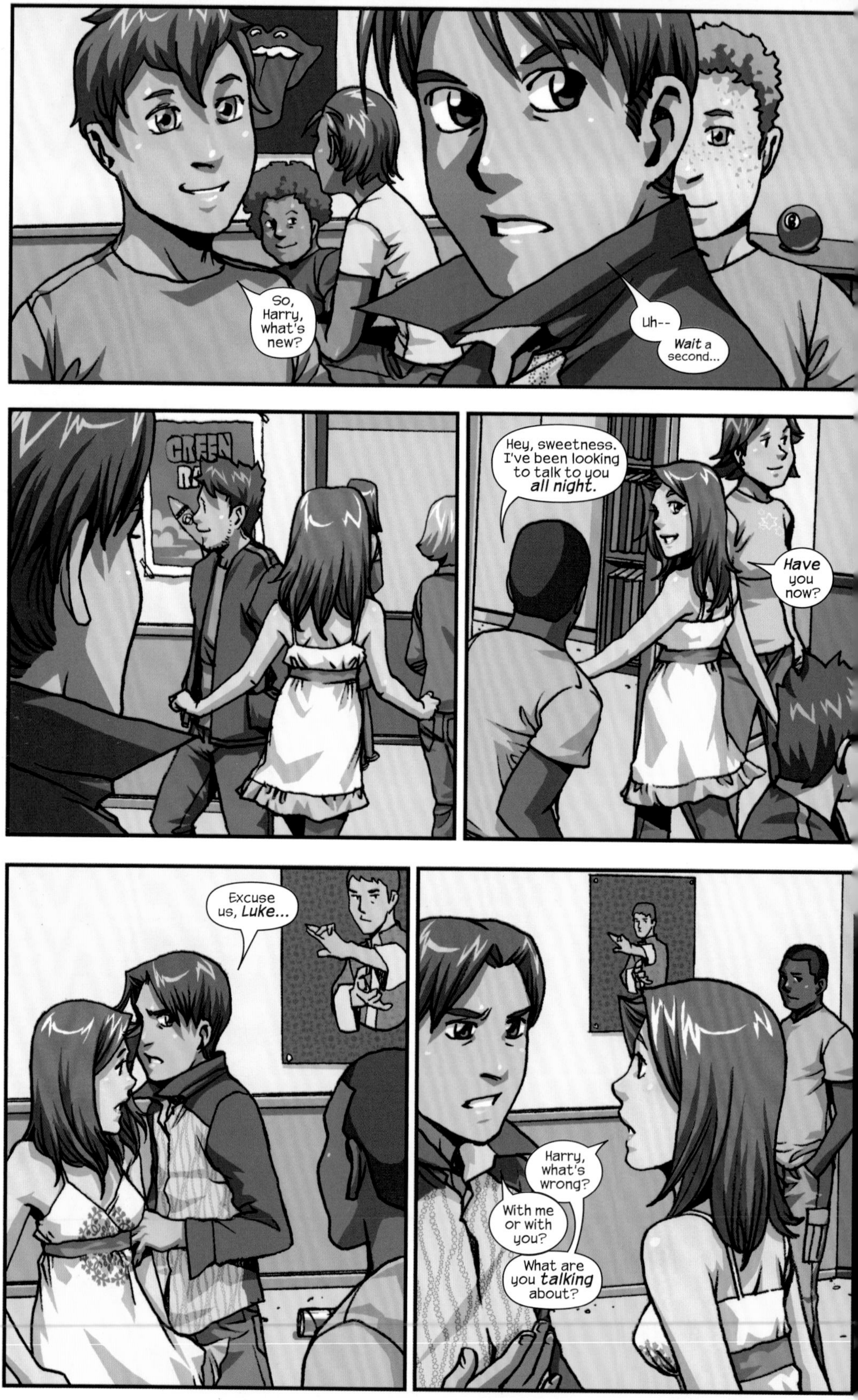
So, Harry, what's new?
Uh--
Wait a second...
GREEN DAY
Hey, sweetness. I've been looking to talk to you all night.
Have you now?
Excuse us, Luke...
Harry, what's wrong?
With me or with you?
What are you talking about?

MJ, you just pulled a *ditch move* on me! I know, because I *use* that move all the *time!*

But I haven't talked to you in *weeks.* I thought, you know--

I wanted to know how you're *doing* and stuff.

Oh, come on, Harry-- I didn't *mean* anything. It's just we see each other *every day.*

It's a *party!* I need to circulate!

Aw, Harry...

I'll talk to you *tomorrow,* okay? At school!

Now, where did we leave off...?

Have you *seen* her lately?

Seen her, yeah. But *talk* to her?

What's her *deal?*

I mean, she used to be my--

I used to *date* her, you know? And now it's like--

Like you're just whoever.

Yeah! Like, "take a *number,* Harry Osborn"!

Liz says she's been like that about a couple *weeks* now.

Seriously? But why?

What happened *two weeks ago?*

Maybe your puny little *friend* there knows.

Yeah, that's right! I *see* ya, *Parker!*

Oh. Good for you.

What is going **ON** up in that head of yours?

Heh, I'm just **teasing** you, Peter. You're so cute when you think I'm actually **serious** about that stuff.

No, I knew you were joking.

Uh-huh...

So, what are we gonna do tonight?

Well... Has there ever been somebody in your life who's, like, the **bane** of your existence and yet, somehow, at the same time you find that person kind of...**amusing**?

Yeah. And I'm **looking** at him right now.

I thought maybe we could go see a movie. I mean, I have no idea what's playing, but there's gotta be **something** decent, right?

I have a better idea. Why don't we **rent** a movie...

...which we can then watch over at **my** place?

Peter... people *KNOW* we're a couple, you know.

I know...

Why are you so *shy* about holding hands in public? Are you *embarrassed?*

Gwen, of *course* not...

Ohmygosh.

You're embarrassed by *me,* aren't you?

No. That is definitely *not true,* and if I make you *feel* that way, then I *promise* you, I'll--

JAVA JOY!

HAHA HAHAHA HA!

Ahehh...

I'm sorry, Peter. I couldn't *help* it!

I'll stop teasing you like that, I *swear...*

Riiight...

Thanks, Jason.

My pleasure, darlin'.

HEY MARY JANE!

Wait! No, not "hi"! I meant come over!

Huh. That's weird...

I know I haven't known Mary Jane for very *long*, but...she hasn't really been *herself* lately, has she?

No, she hasn't. Not since...

Not since what?

What?

Oh. Uh...

Well, the *last* time I talked to her--a couple weeks ago? She came to my house. Said she had something *important* to tell me.

What was it?

She, uh... she said she was really happy for us.

For you and me, I mean.

And then she said she had to go and...she left.

Really? She said that?

Aww...! She's so awesome.

Isn't she awesome?

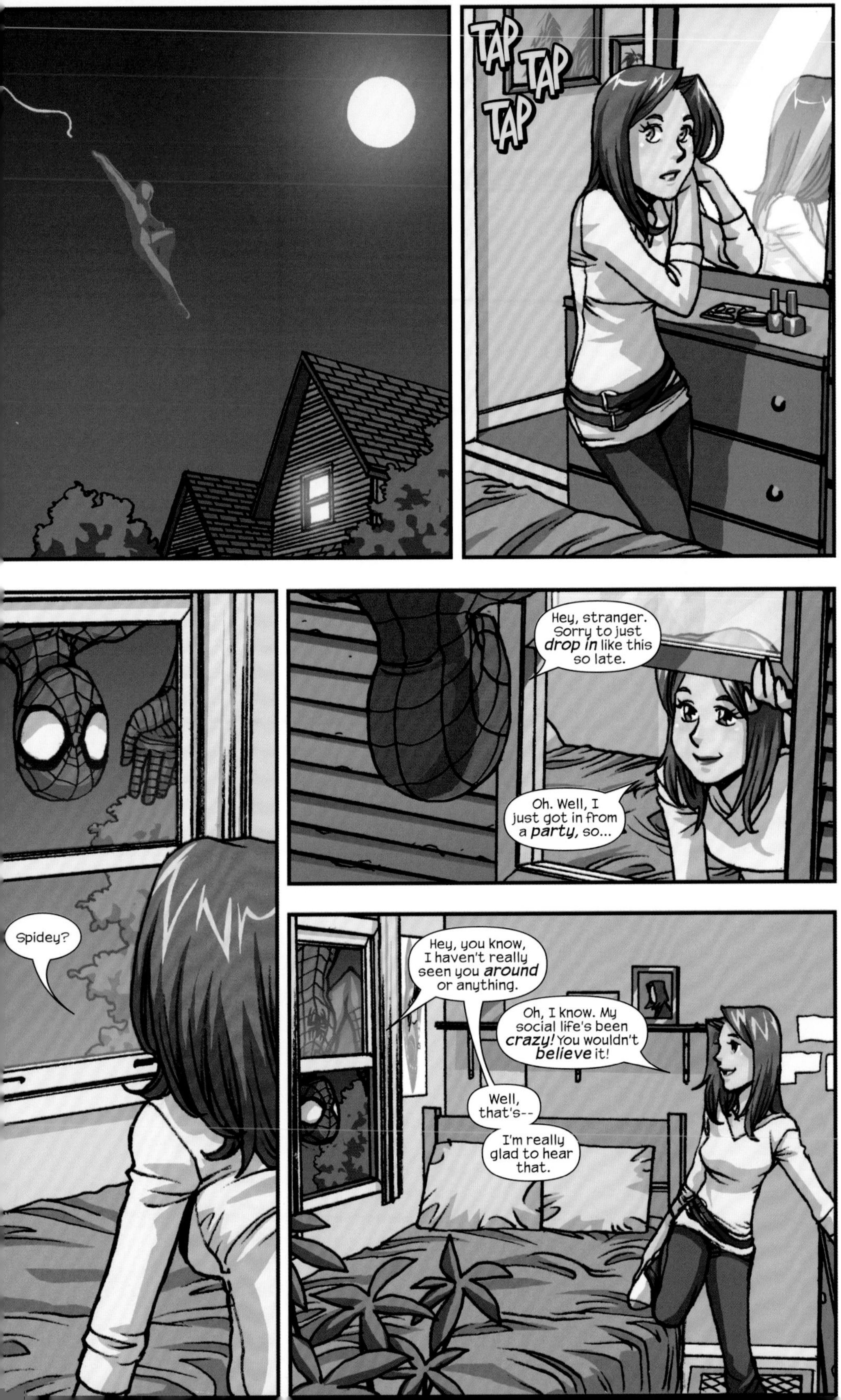

TAP TAP TAP
Spidey?
Hey, stranger. Sorry to just drop in like this so late.
Oh. Well, I just got in from a party, so...
Hey, you know, I haven't really seen you around or anything.
Oh, I know. My social life's been crazy! You wouldn't believe it!
Well, that's--
I'm really glad to hear that.

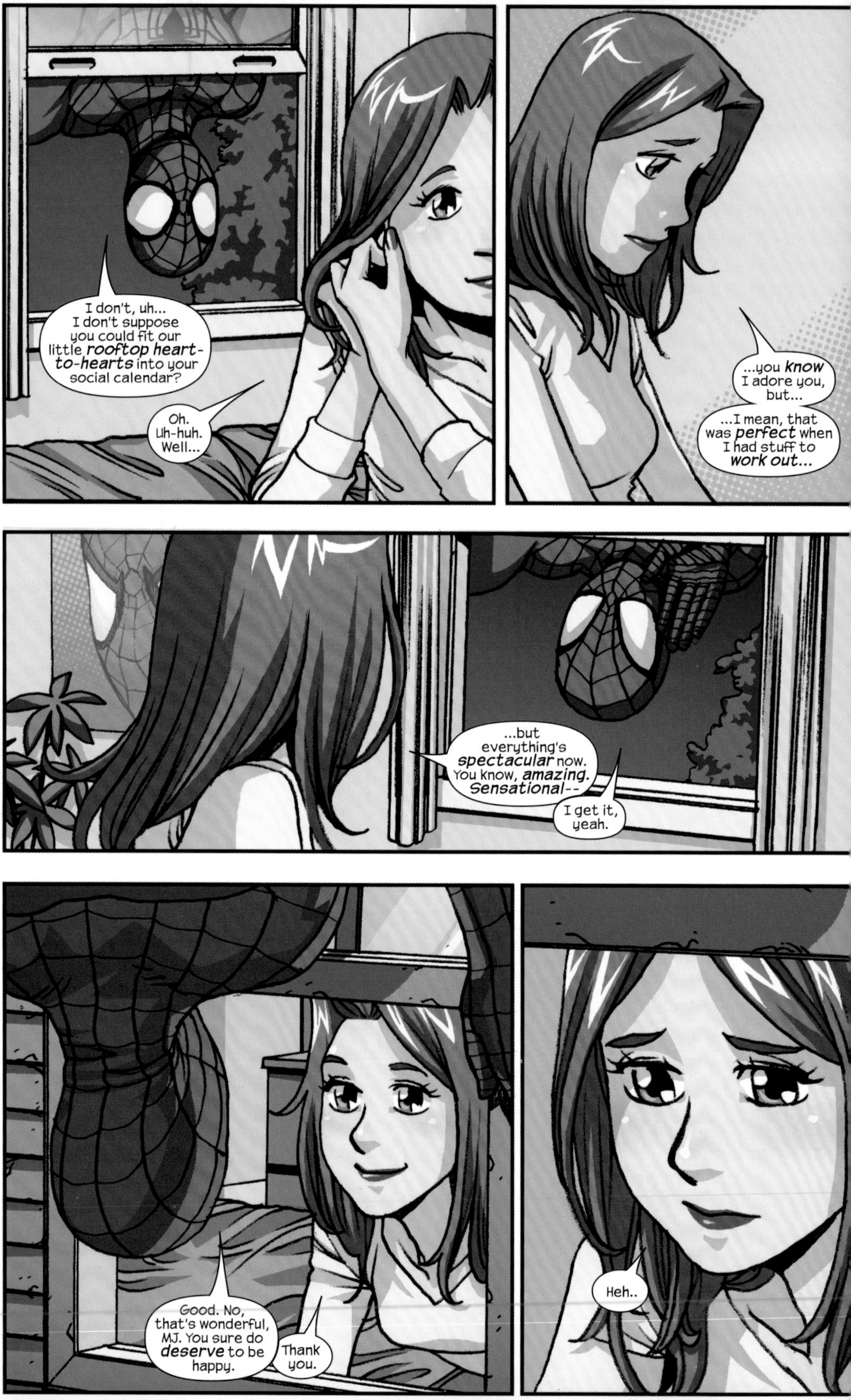
I don't, uh... I don't suppose you could fit our little rooftop heart-to-hearts into your social calendar?
Oh. Uh-huh. Well...
...you know I adore you, but...
...I mean, that was perfect when I had stuff to work out...
...but everything's spectacular now. You know, amazing. Sensational--
I get it, yeah.
Good. No, that's wonderful, MJ. You sure do deserve to be happy.
Thank you.
Heh..

Well, I guess, uh...I guess I'll see you around, then.

Ouch.

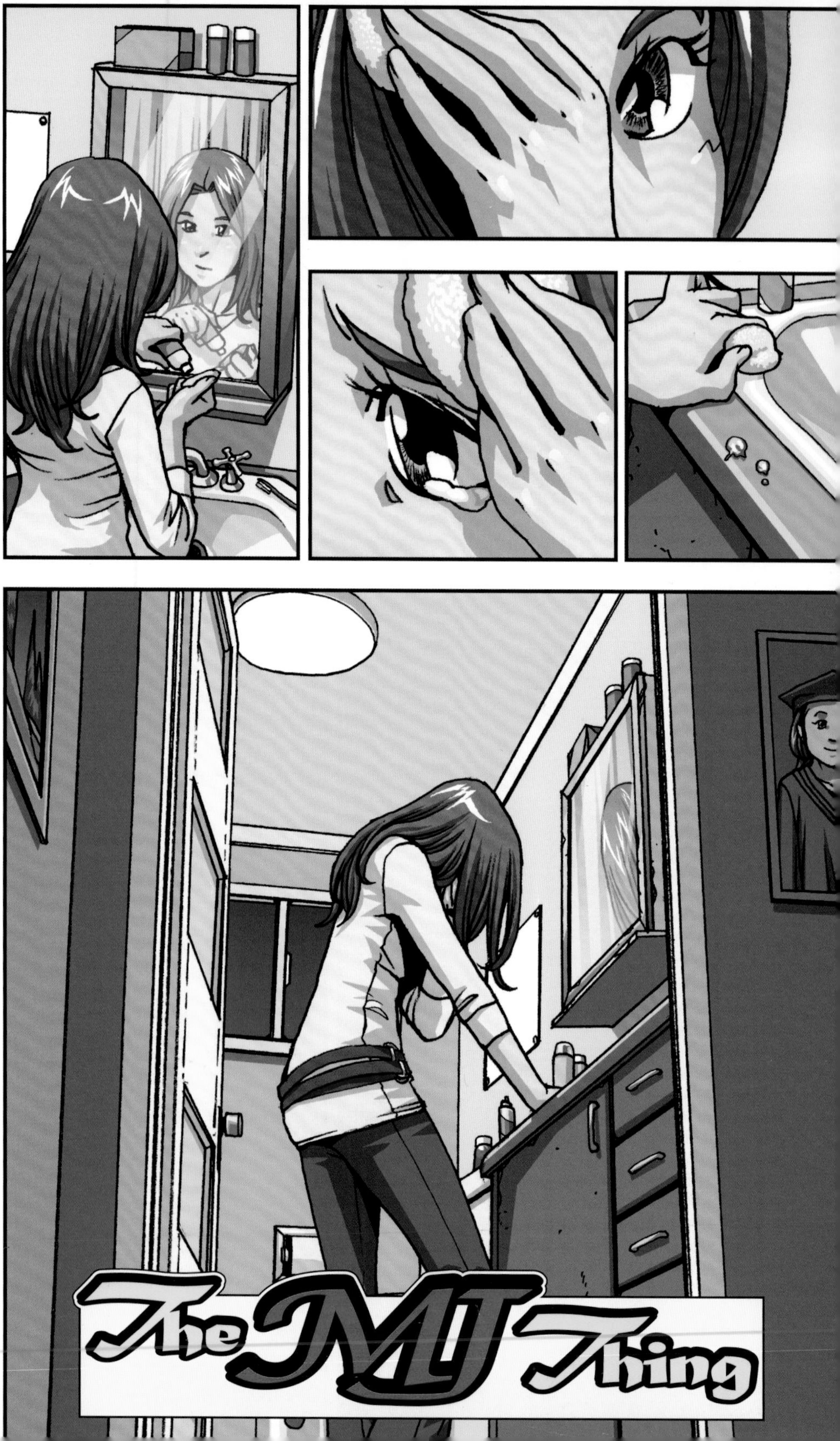
The MJ Thing

Spider-Man Loves Mary Jane #12

Can
I help
you?

Hi. Joy
Mercado.

With
the *Midtown
Magnifier*?

The
school
paper?

My editor
spoke with
you, right?

No?

Okay, well...

I'm doing a piece on the nature of being *superficially amorous*? We took an informal *poll* on who the student body thought was the biggest male and female *flirt*.

It *probably* doesn't surprise you that you topped the list. I'd like to talk to you about it, if that's okay.

What, right now?

It can be whenever you want.

So...you'd be telling the whole *school* what I say.

If it's on the record, yeah. But anything *off* the record I'll hold in the *strictest* confidence.

Of course, if you're not *interested*, that's cool, too. I'll just go to the *number two guy*...

Come on, now--no need to *play* me.

Sounds kinda fun. I'll do it.

Great. Let me know when's a good *time* for you and we can--

Hang on a sec.

Who was the number one *female*?

MJ, hi. Wow, when was the last time we--?

I realized we haven't spoken in a while, so--

I'll be honest with you. I'm kinda worried about--

Really, guys...

...I didn't need *two* of you to carry my books for me, but thanks anyway.

Hey MJ!

Hey *yourself*, Mister Osborn.

Uh, yeah. So, uh...did you talk to the *paper* yet?

Oh, the *flirting* thing? Well, they *told* me about it, but there's no way I'll actually *do* it.

Right. Of course.

YEARBOOK

Um...why, exactly?

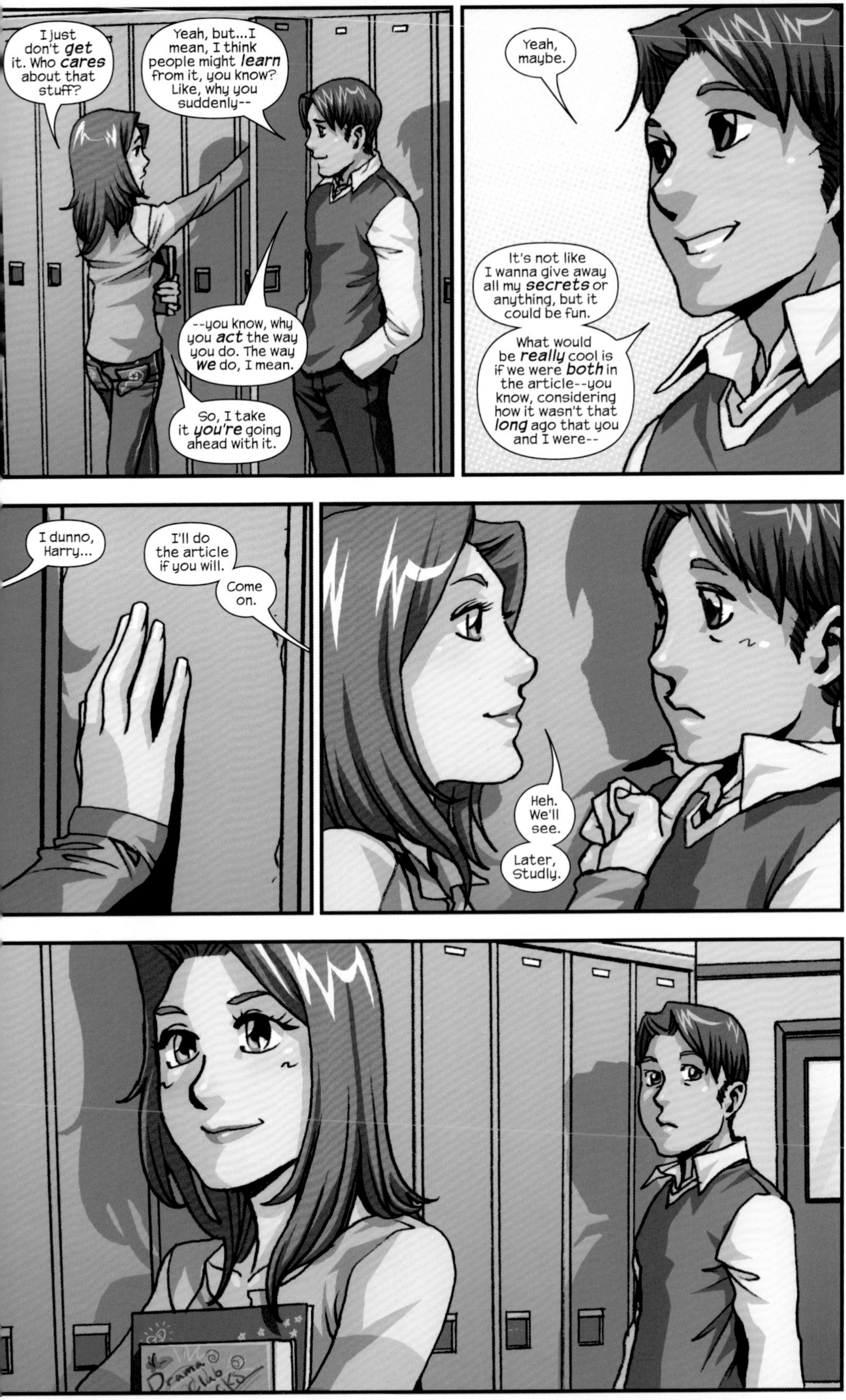
I just don't get it. Who cares about that stuff?
Yeah, but...I mean, I think people might learn from it, you know? Like, why you suddenly--
--you know, why you act the way you do. The way we do, I mean.
So, I take it you're going ahead with it.
Yeah, maybe.
It's not like I wanna give away all my secrets or anything, but it could be fun.
What would be really cool is if we were both in the article--you know, considering how it wasn't that long ago that you and I were--
I dunno, Harry...
I'll do the article if you will.
Come on.
Heh. We'll see.
Later, Studly.
Drama Club

'Sup, MJ.

⊰Guhh!⊱

⊰HFF...⊱
Who knew going plastic would be so *exhausting?*

Did you... lose a *contact* or something?

Well? Given it any more thought?

I *thought* you were going to the second girl on the list.

I was bluffing. It's gotta be *you*, Mary Jane.

Please? Without you, the article's *worthless.* And it'll be fun! I swear.

You're not going to give up, are you?

Is that a "yes"?

Hhh...

...yes.

Rock!

How about sixth period? You have *study hall* then.

You know my *schedule?*

Hey, I'm a journalist!

Well, I've got *homework* today, so...

Tomorrow it is!

See you then!

You've **gotta** tell me, Liz--

--what is the **deal** with her?

More like, "what **isn't** the deal with her"?

What does that **mean**?

No idea. It just sounded appropriately snarky.

Look, best I can figure, she's running from her feelings for--

--she's just running from her feelings, period. You **know** how she is.

It's never been like **this**. What happened that was so bad?

Ask her.

You know I can't **do** that, Liz. She and I aren't--

You're her best friend. Are you telling me you don't know?

I'm telling you I'm **not** telling you, Harry. If she wants you to know...you'll know. You know?

Pft...fine, whatever.

So, you're back together with *Flash*?

We worked things out between us, yeah.

You should try to do the same.

Are you out of your mind? I'll still *small-talk* with him, but there's *no way* I'll--

I mean, *he* tells my girlfriend he's in *love* with her, and somehow *I* wind up in the doghouse. Explain *that* one to me.

If Flash never said that stuff to MJ, we'd *still* be going out.

Wait, are you saying you wanna--?

No! I'm not--

I'm not.

It's just the principle of the thing, that's all.

I'm going to start recording now.

Okay?

Fire away.

Okay. So...

...what would you say are the hallmark *traits* of a flirt?

Kindness... um, empathy...

A great bod and a *killer* smile.

...self-confidence?

You definitely have to *believe* in yourself. You have to *know* you're what girls want.

And what do you think gives you the level of self-confidence *required* to be a flirt?

It comes from...*other people*, I guess.

You know, when you...catch a guy checking you out, or I guess when a girl *sneers* at you? That sort of thing.

Beats me. *Whatever* it is, I just *have* it. I've *always* had it.

Maybe what *you* have isn't so much *self-confidence* as it is *arrogance*.

I'm sorry-- is that a *question*?

Mary Jane, your *answers*... if you don't mind my saying, they tend to be, well... *conveniently* tame.

Did you maybe *prepare* your comments in advance?

I don't know what you mean.

Thing is, I can't help but wonder if you're... *avoiding* some-thing.

Now look, I thought this was gonna be a simple *interview,* not *character assassination.*

I don't do *fluff.*

You have to understand, Harry, that there's something more *important* to a journalist than mere *answers.*

Like what?

The. *truth.*

CEBULSKI RULES!!

ZIWEE 4 PREZ!

Right. Okay.

This interview?

It's *over.*

Joy, if you came to *apologize*--

Apologize? I came to find out when we can finish our interview.

After the way you tried to *sabotage* me yesterday?

Look, I promise I won't be so *invasive* this time.

Right. I believe *that*...

Thing is, Mary Jane...

...if you *won't* talk to me? I'll have no choice but to print how you *stormed off* like some *über-*sensitive diva.

And I'm *sure* you don't want that.

Now...could we *please* finish what we started?

Luke, you're too much...!

Can you *believe* her?!

Hmm?

Joy Mercado! She's a *viper!*

I actually walked *out* on her interview, and then she's all, "if you don't *play ball* I'm gonna *skewer* you in the *school paper!*"

She did the same thing to me.

I *figured* as much.

Look, I say we stand our ground-- be, like, a *unified front?* Go to her advisors and *tell* them what passes for *journalism* around here. Tell them how she basically tried to *blackmail* us.

And then Joy Mercado can *shove* her story--

What? What's that look for?

You're *with* me, aren't you?

Oh, man... did you finish the interview?

You finished the interview.

What did you tell her?

What she wanted to hear.

So you *lied* to her.

Basically, yeah.

I told her this whole thing about how I'm just *addicted* to the *attention*, blah, blah, blah...

Why would you *say* that? It makes you sound so *shallow*.

MJ, it's almost as bad as whatever she would have *made up!*

I *realize* that now, but... I was just so desperate to get her off my back...!

Look, can we not talk about this anymore? It's a party! We're *supposed* to be *partying*.

Come here.

Harry, what--?

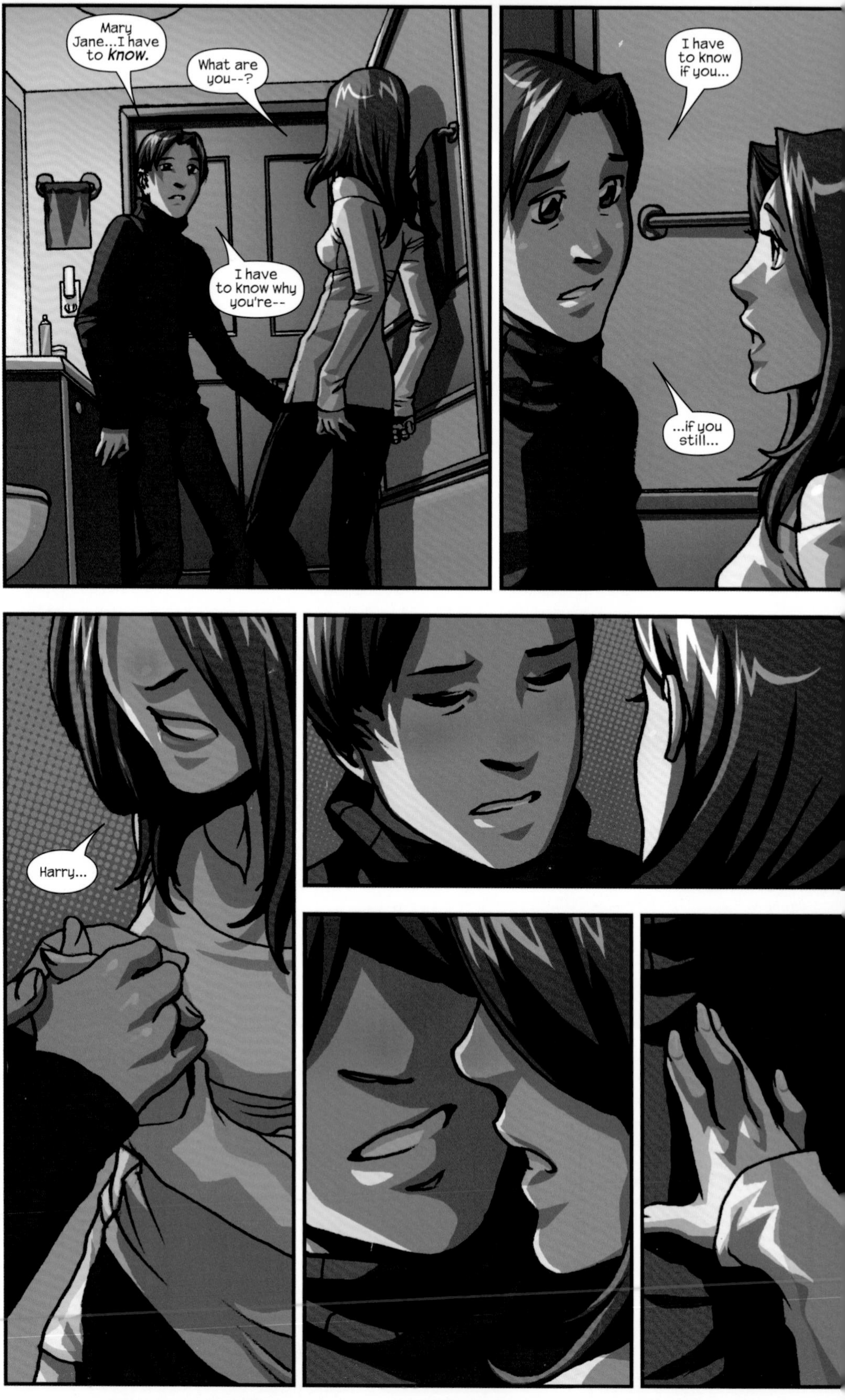
Mary Jane...I have to *know.*
What are you--?
I have to know why you're--
I have to know if you...
...if you still...
Harry...

Harry Osborn, you *goober*. You crack me up.

Mmwah.

Come on, Romeo. Time to actually *enjoy* the festivities!

Well...what do you have for me?

The truth. That's what you *wanted,* right?

Yeah...

Why do I get the feeling there's a catch?

I get final edit on *anything* you write about Mary Jane.

Not a chance. That isn't how it *works,* Harry. I refuse to compromise my--

Stop, okay? You wouldn't know *journalistic integrity* if it walked up and *introduced* itself.

And anyway, this *isn't* a negotiation. Take it or leave it.

Come on, Joy.

You *know* that what I have to say is gonna be juicier than whatever non-sense you *coerced* out of MJ...

Would it be a fair assessment to say you're *arrogant*?

I can see why people might *think* that of me.

Can you?

I'm charismatic. Confident. Happy. I've got a lot going for me.

You're happy?

Absolutely. Why *wouldn't* I be?

You tell me.

Heh... you're something else.

What do you get *out* of being a flirt?

I like the *chase*. The affection, the excitement...

Once you start dating someone *exclusively,* all that goes away.

Don't you ever want anything *more* than base infatuation?

I like your eyes.

Don't change the subject.

Have you ever felt anything more than just *attracted*? You and *Mary Jane Watson* seem to--

Why do you keep *dancing around* like this? Why don't you ask what you *really* wanna know? Why I do it?

That's what I *get* out of it. It isn't *why.*

You *told* me already-- the chase.

Well... why *do* you do it?

I like to be a flirt because...

...because...

You know, you were right. I *was* just trying to change the subject before, but...

I've always been *intimidated* by smart girls...but there's just something *about* you. Some inner fire...this perfect, like... energy...

You're not funny.

Joy, look at me. I'm not trying to be. You *know* that, don't you?

But I'm just a--

You're not "just" anything, Joy Mercado...

I do it, Joy...

...because I can.

YOU AWFUL--!

Harry Osborn and Mary Jane Watson, please report to the front office.

Awesome! You're both here.

Sorry about pulling you from class, *especially* since Joy says she's not going to do her little *flirting* exposé after all.

Still, the *chief* says we *need* a pic to go with it--you know, just in case.

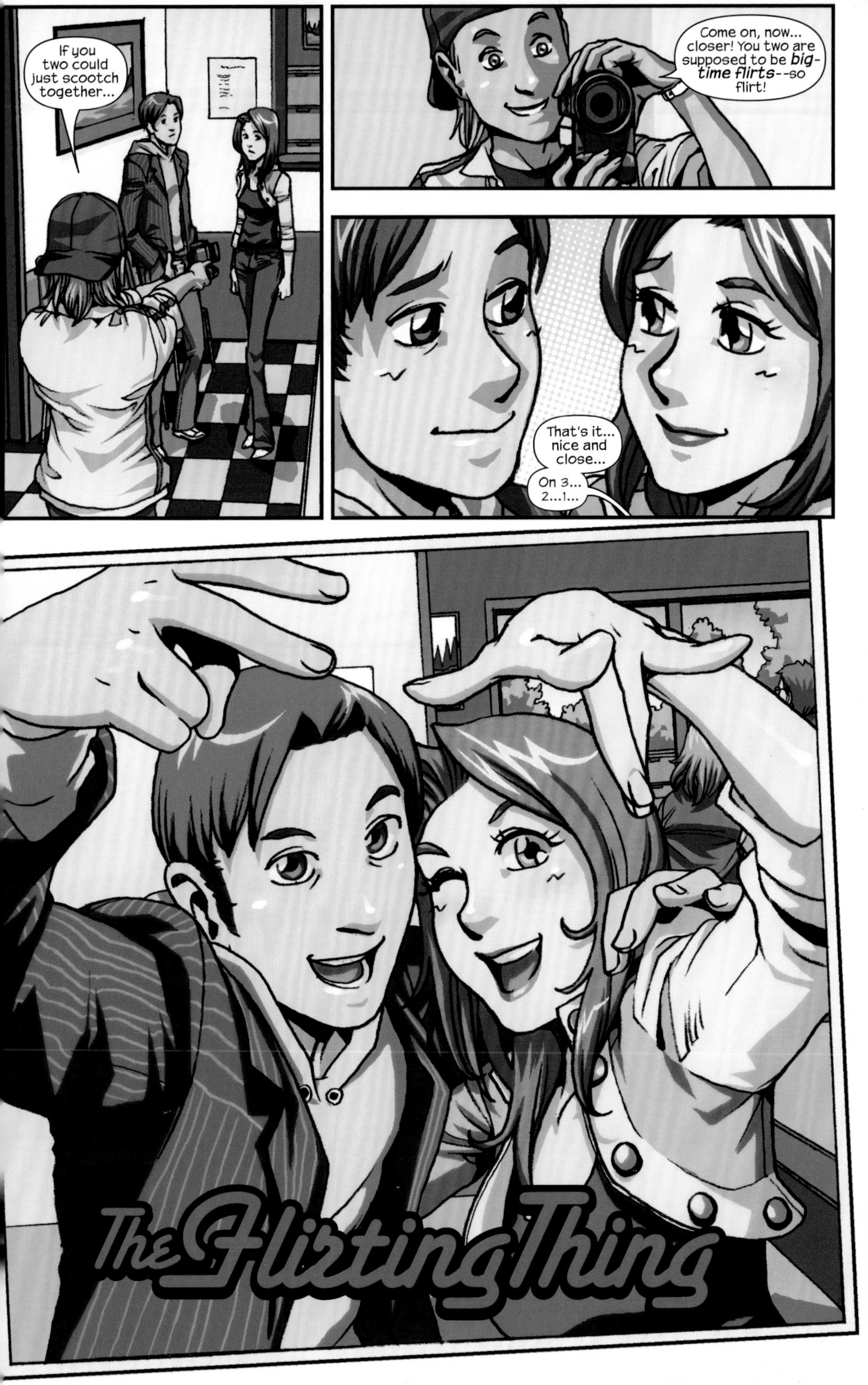
If you two could just scootch together...
Come on, now... closer! You two are supposed to be *big-time flirts*--so flirt!
That's it... nice and close...
On 3... 2...1...
The Flirting Thing

Spider-Man Loves Mary Jane #13

Oh!

Hi, guys.

How's it goin', MJ?

Flawlessly. And yourself...?

Wow.

Definitely not alone at lunch *this* time, huh?

This isn't your lunch period, Gwen...

Yeah...I skipped so I could *talk* to you.

It's kinda *personal?* And I was hoping--

Boy, I dunno, Gwen. I'd *hate* to be rude to all these *guests...*

It doesn't have to be right now! It can be whenever you want. I just really need--

Please, Mary Jane. Could you *please* talk to me?

You're the only other friend I *have* here.

Two spinach 'n' pep!

Hope you like it. It's the closest thing to Montoni's downtown. I *loved* that place...

I had to shuffle my whole *dance card* around for this...

Mm. I *really* appreciate it. I know you've been so *crazy popular* lately.

Thing is, Mary Jane...

...I think I'm having a real problem with *Peter*.

Peter.

Yeah. You know, Peter *Parker*? Your friend? My *boyfriend*?

I guess I thought since you probably know him better than *anyone else* in school, you'd be able to help.

Peter's so adorable and stuff, but...I just can't figure him out. One second, we'll be having all the fun in the world...

...and then all of a sudden he remembers that he forgot to lock his *house door.* Or he left a *burner* on in chemistry. Or his *aunt* asked him to buy *groceries.*

It's like he's *avoiding* something. Like...he's avoiding *me.*

It's *definitely* not you, Gwen. It was always the same with me when we were--

You know, when we were study partners and stuff.

Yeah, but *why?*

I kinda chalked it up to his being an *orphan,* and then losing the uncle who *raised* him on top of that.

Did he tell you about--?

Yeah.

Well, there's that. Plus, he's got that whole *absentminded professor* thing going on, you know? He can be such a *scatterbrain* sometimes!

Yeah...

Yeah.

But I guess, to be honest...

...I never really tried to figure it out beyond my first impressions.

Why not? Didn't it bother you?

Well...not *at first*, I guess, because we were just *study partners*.

Then we became friends...

...and it *still* didn't matter, simply because when he was around-- when he was *paying attention*--

Anyway, it is *not* you. So breathe easy, okay?

Wait, what're you--?

I gotta run. Hot date!

I don't know, Spidey...

I don't know how long I can keep this up.

I wanna help her, I *do*, but...I mean, how am I supposed to be my new, carefree self when I'm talking about *serious stuff* like that?

Not to *mention* the person and relationship she wants to *talk* about are the *reasons* I put up all these walls in the *first* place!

It's like, either way, no matter what I do...it's *gonna* sting.

And the *worst* part is, I could *probably* work all this out if I had someone else to *confess* all this to!

Well? Aren't you gonna say anything?

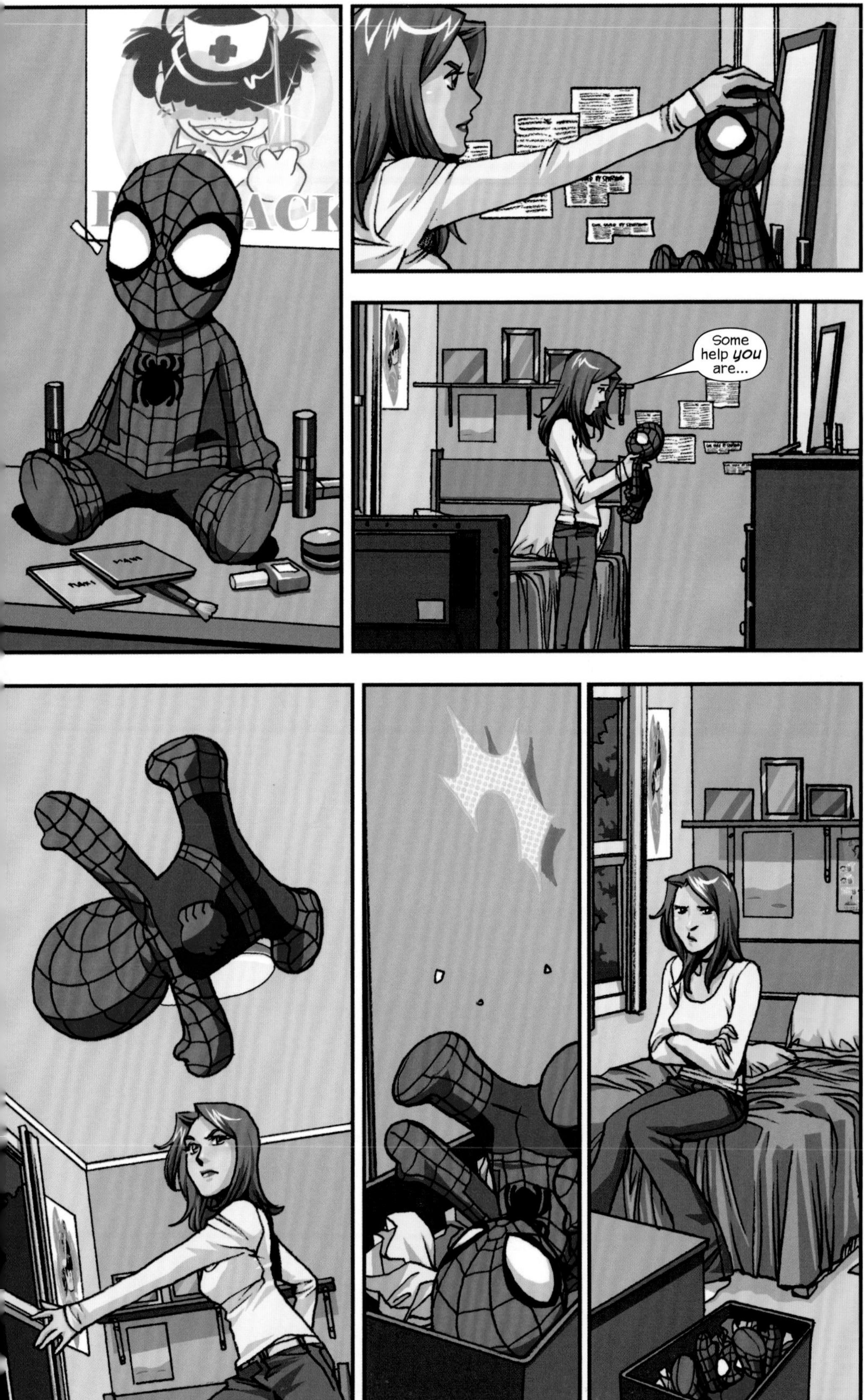
Some help *you* are...

...wasn't *my* fault I tripped. Maybe if you didn't wear that *hair clip* all the time, you wouldn't be so darn *distracting.*

Peter Parker! Did you just *flirt* with me?

Oh. Huh. I guess I did, didn't I?

You know that means I'm getting *used* to you, right? Better make your *escape plans* while you still--

BREAKING NEWS: HULK RAMPAGES IN NY

Oh, man.

I just remembered...I've gotta pick up Aunt May's *meds* from the pharmacy.

Okay, no biggie. We'll just--

Sorry, Gwen, but it's *gotta* be *right now.*

Fine, but I don't see why I can't--

If she doesn't take her refill in time, *she'll be very angry!*

I'll call you!

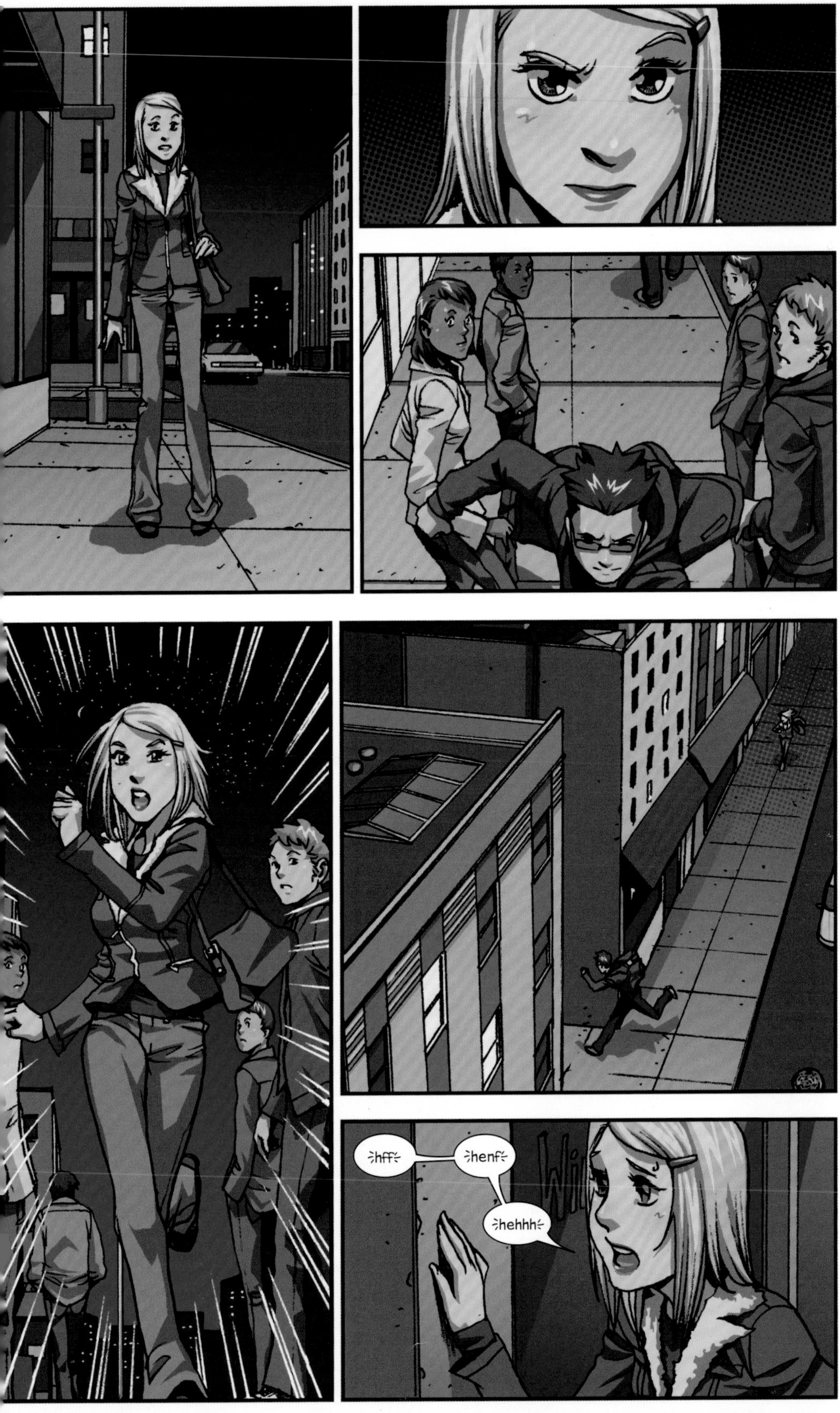
hff
henf
hehhh

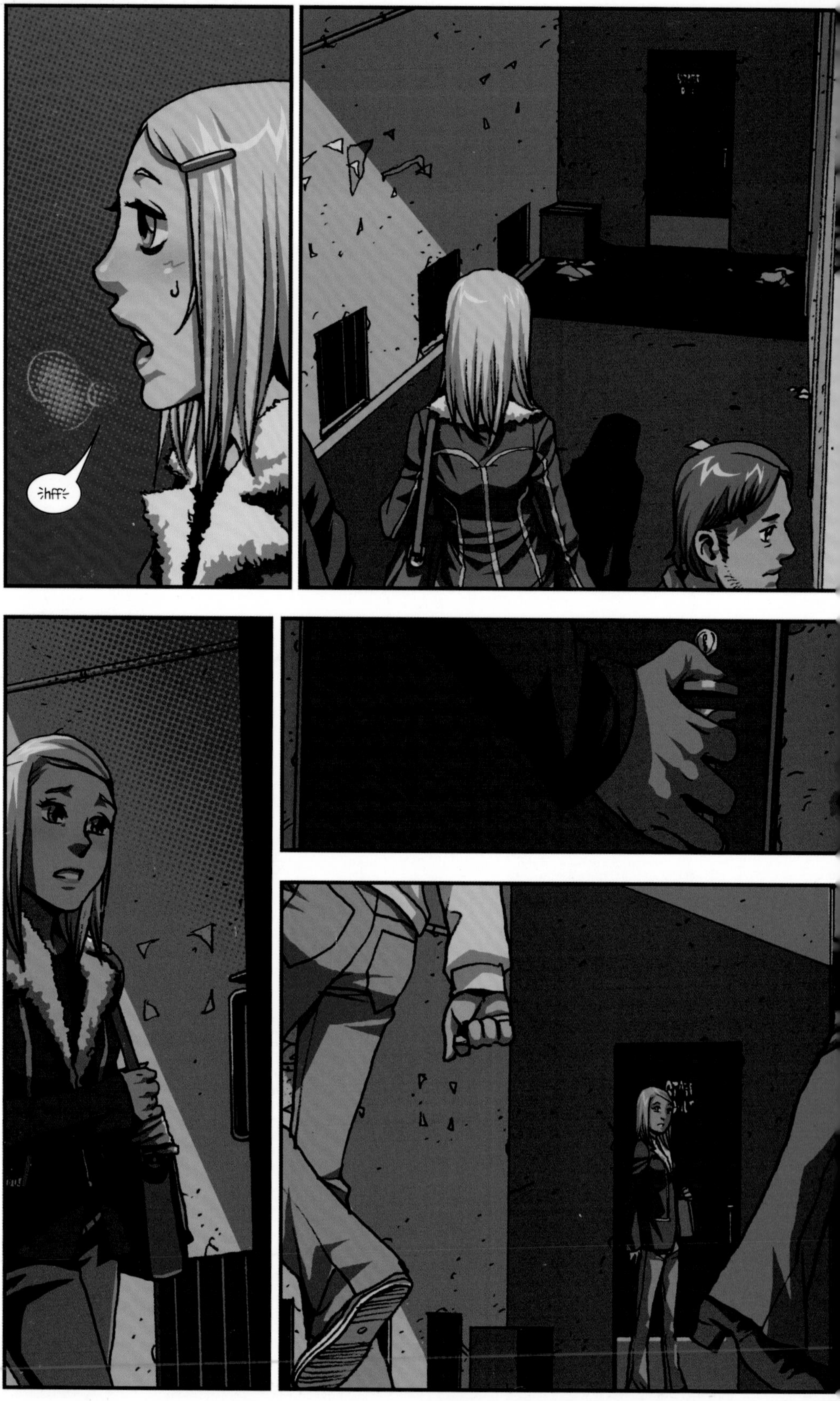
hff

...and you know *what else*? I called his *aunt*, and she didn't know anything *about* any medication refills!

Hey, guys...

He's *your* boyfriend. Why don't you just *ask* him?

You don't think I've *tried* that? He *acts* like he has no idea what I'm talking about! He changes the subject!

Well, I don't know what you expect *me* to do about it.

I need your *help*, Mary Jane! It's driving me *nuts!*

And you're driving *me* nuts, Gwen!

Do you honestly think I *care* about what Peter Parker does or doesn't do?

W-well, actually, I--

Can't you just *leave me alone?!*

Uchh. Great.

I'm a jerk.

BRRRRRINNG!
BRRRRRINNG!

Uh...Gwen? Look, before you say anything, I just wanted to--

Mary Jane! Mary Jane!

You won't *believe* what just happened!

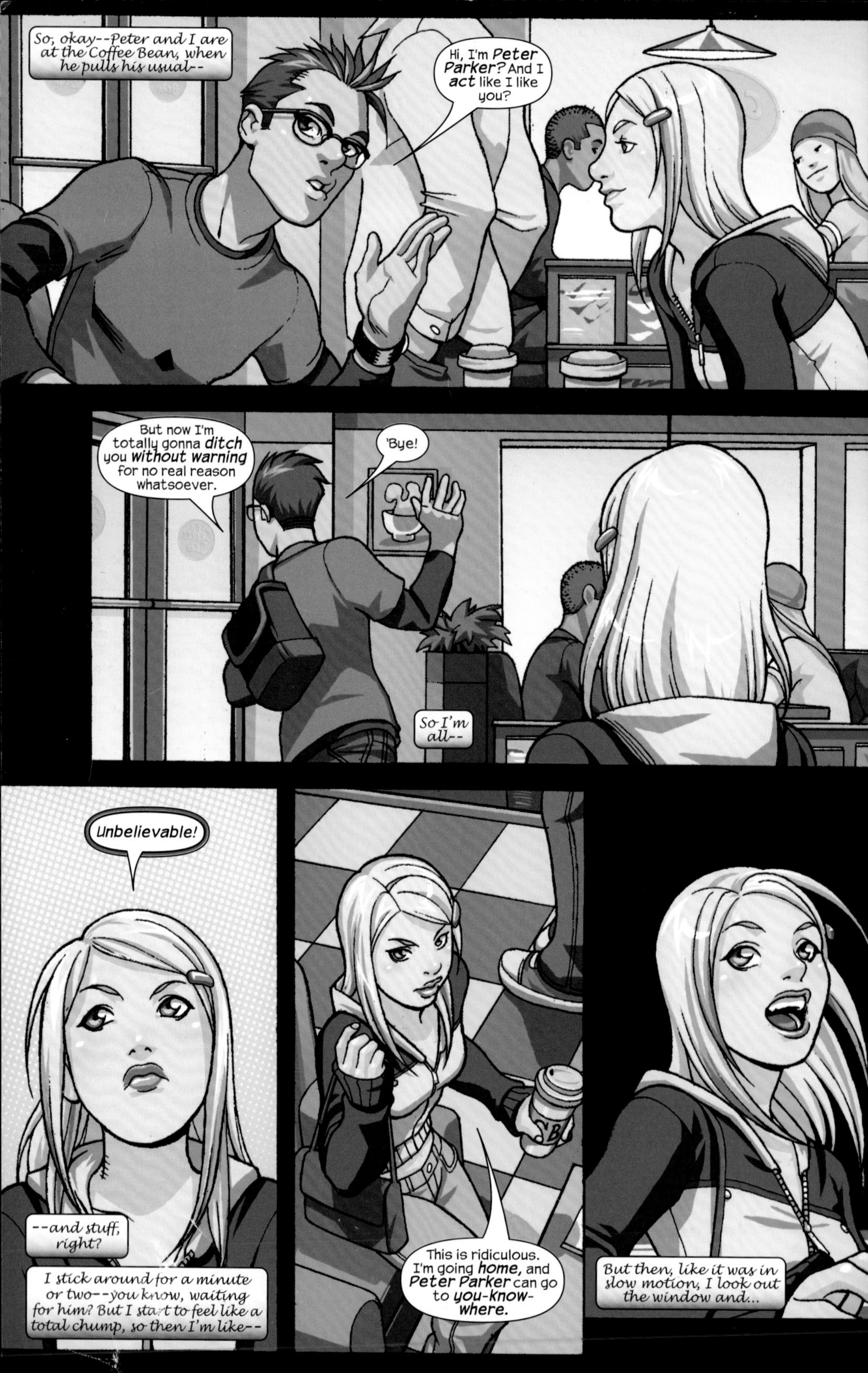

So, okay--Peter and I are at the Coffee Bean, when he pulls his usual--
Hi, I'm Peter Parker? And I act like I like you?
But now I'm totally gonna ditch you without warning for no real reason whatsoever.
'Bye!
So I'm all--
Unbelievable!
--and stuff, right?
I stick around for a minute or two--you know, waiting for him? But I start to feel like a total chump, so then I'm like--
This is ridiculous. I'm going home, and Peter Parker can go to you-know-where.
But then, like it was in slow motion, I look out the window and...

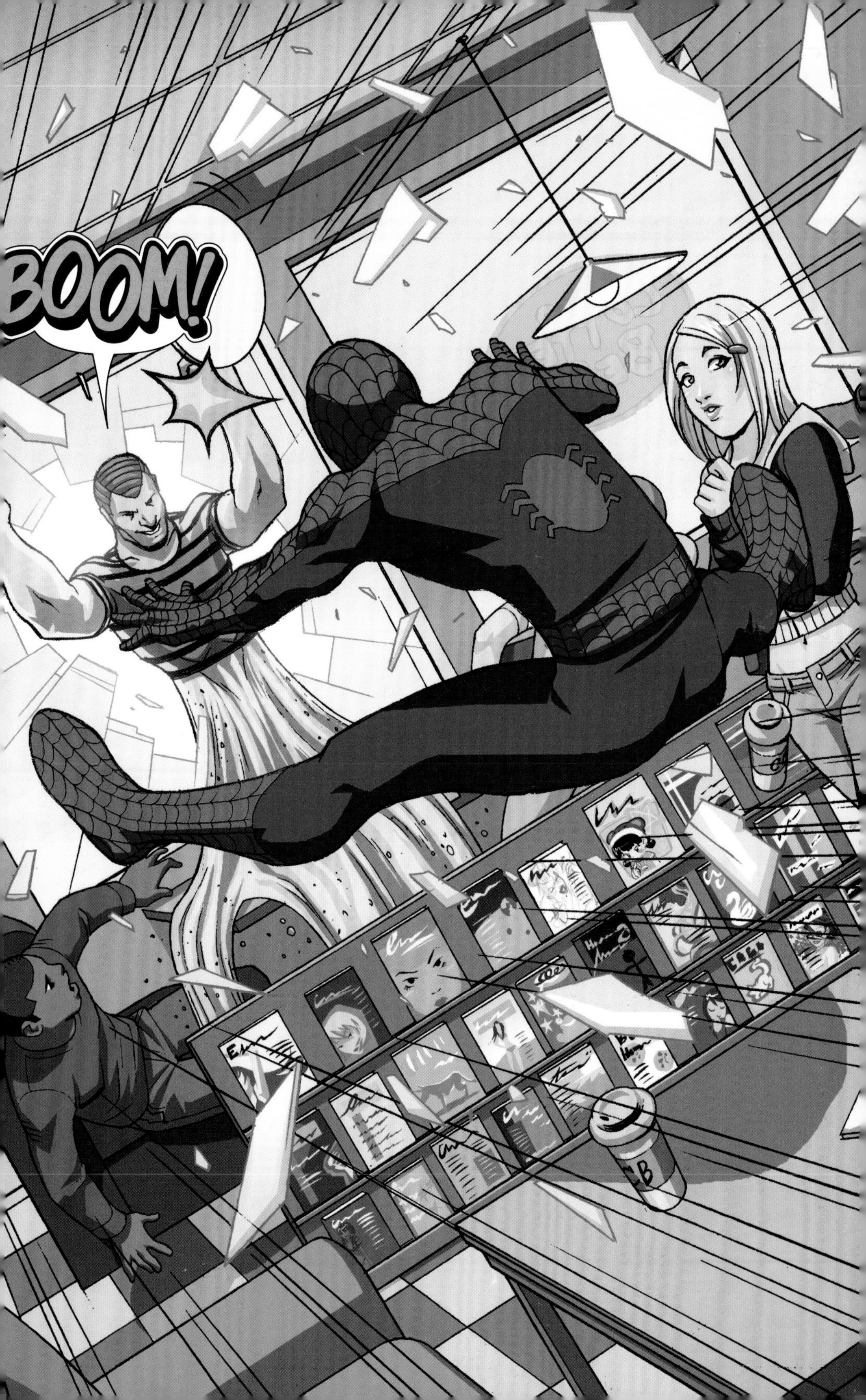
BOOM!

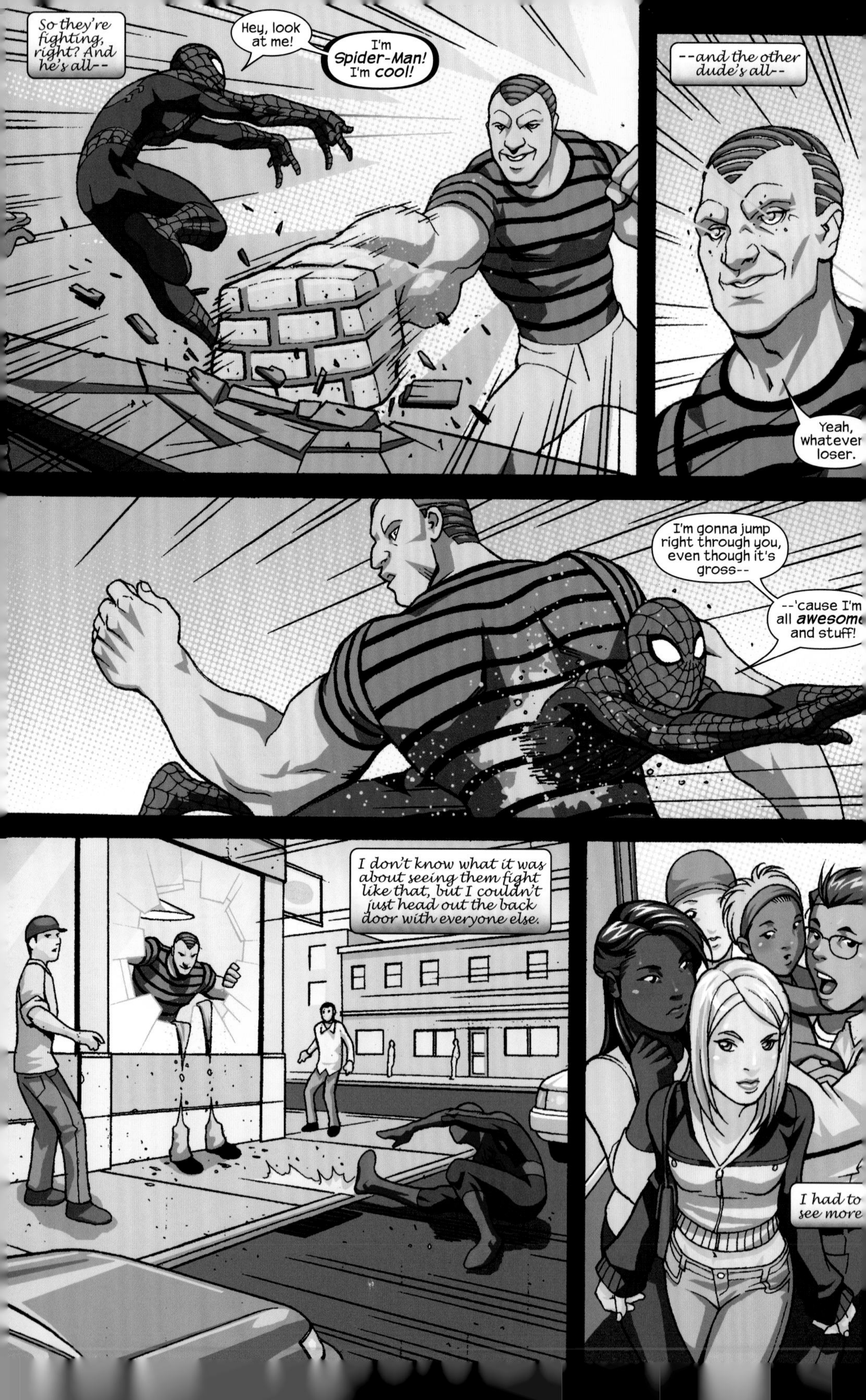
So they're fighting, right? And he's all--
Hey, look at me!
I'm Spider-Man! I'm cool!
--and the other dude's all--
Yeah, whatever loser.
I'm gonna jump right through you, even though it's gross--
--'cause I'm all awesome and stuff!
I don't know what it was about seeing them fight like that, but I couldn't just head out the back door with everyone else.
I had to see more

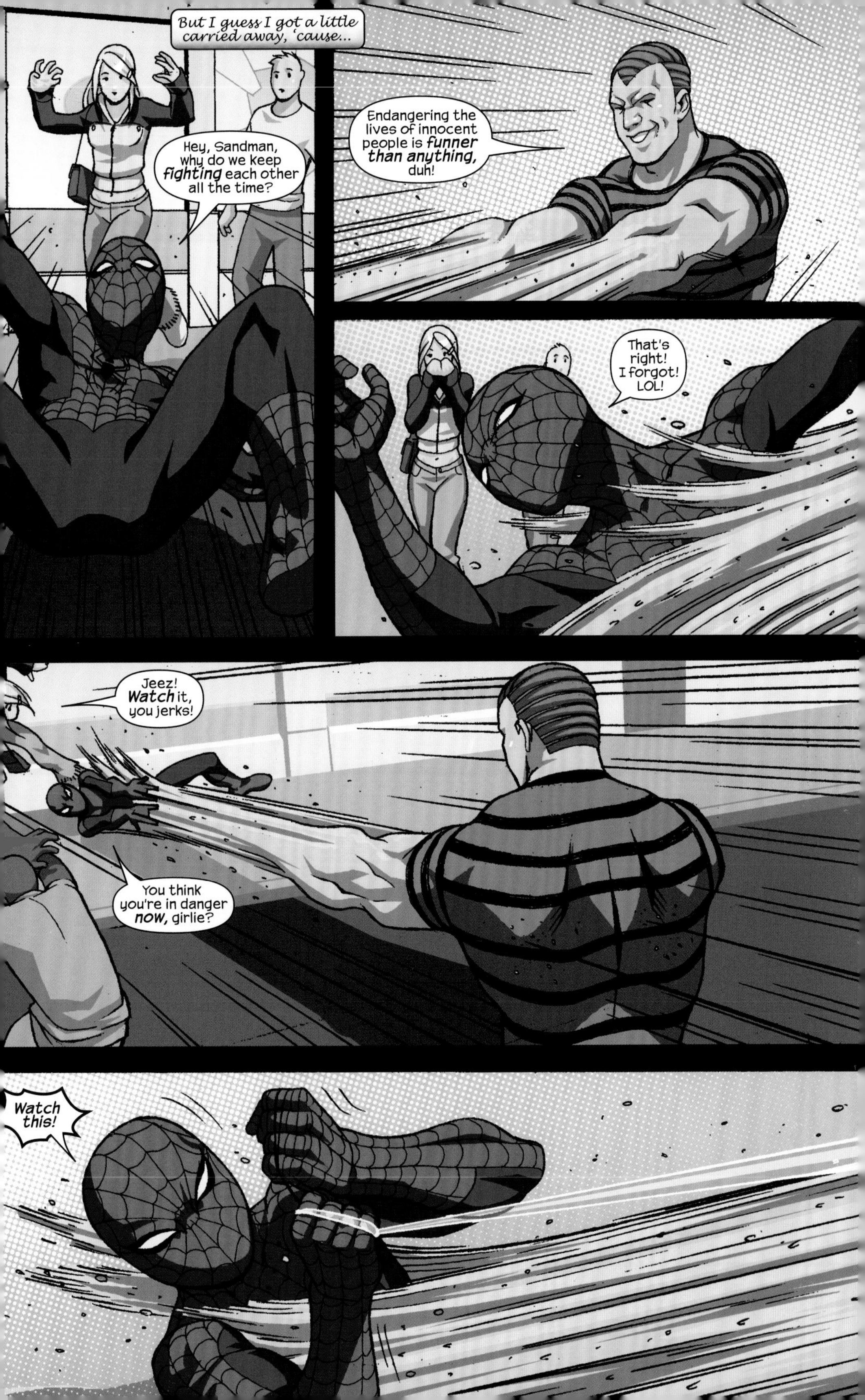
But I guess I got a little carried away, 'cause...
Hey, Sandman, why do we keep *fighting* each other all the time?
Endangering the lives of innocent people is *funner than anything,* duh!
That's right! I forgot! LOL!
Jeez! *Watch* it, you jerks!
You think you're in danger *NOW,* girlie?
Watch this!

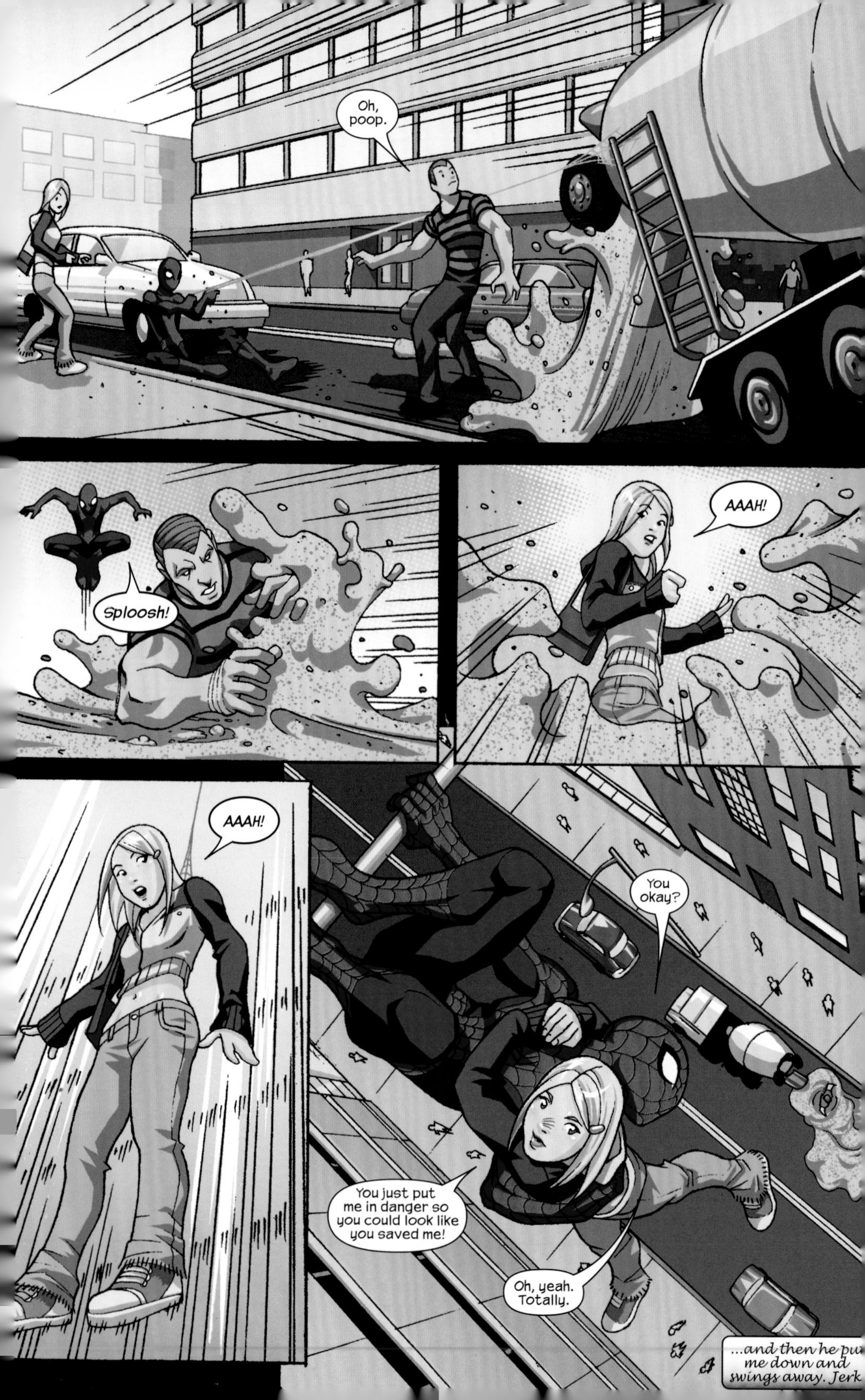
Oh, poop.
Sploosh!
AAAH!
AAAH!
You okay?
You just put me in danger so you could look like you saved me!
Oh, yeah. Totally.
...and then he pu me down and swings away. Jerk

Gwen! Ohmygosh!

So you're *okay*, right?

I *guess* so, yeah, but...

The reason I called? It's because Peter...he's *never around*.

This is it. The last straw. I can't... I can't have him *abandoning* me all the time.

Well, anyway... I just needed to *tell* somebody, so... thanks for listening. And, *really*, don't worry about yesterday. It's okay.

... No, I understand. You can't expect people to always be *patient* with you... you know?

Whoa. What *happened* here?

He's here. I better go.

... 'kay. Thanks.

Gwen, are you all *right*?

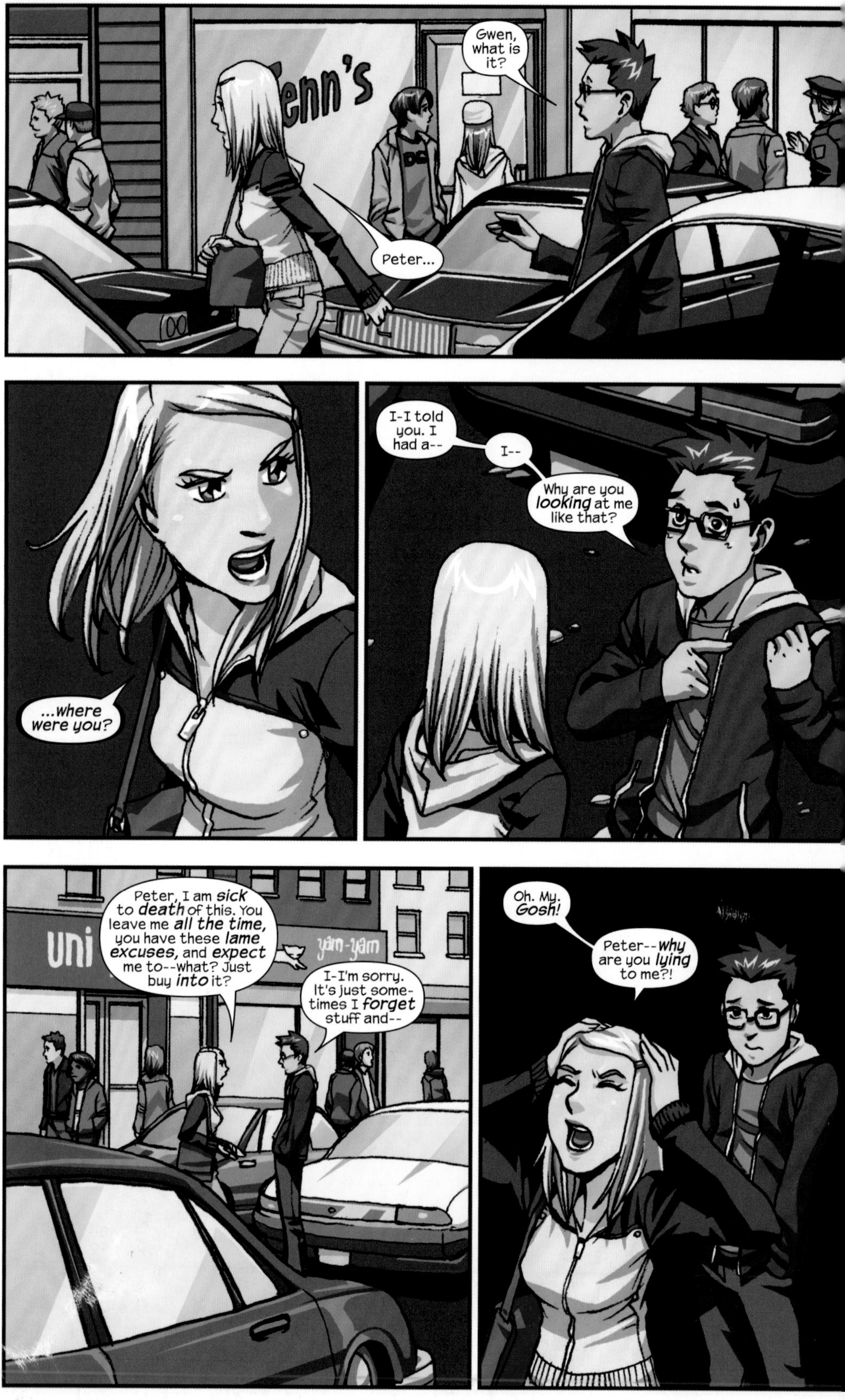
Gwen, what is it?
Peter...
...where were you?
I-I told you. I had a--
I--
Why are you looking at me like that?
Peter, I am sick to death of this. You leave me all the time, you have these lame excuses, and expect me to--what? Just buy into it?
I-I'm sorry. It's just sometimes I forget stuff and--
Oh. My. Gosh!
Peter--why are you lying to me?!

Peter...you have to tell me what's going on, or else...

Or else that's it for us.

I want to tell you, but...

...I shouldn't.

Peter, please.

Whatever it is, you can tell me. You *know* you can.

Okay.

But it has to be our secret.

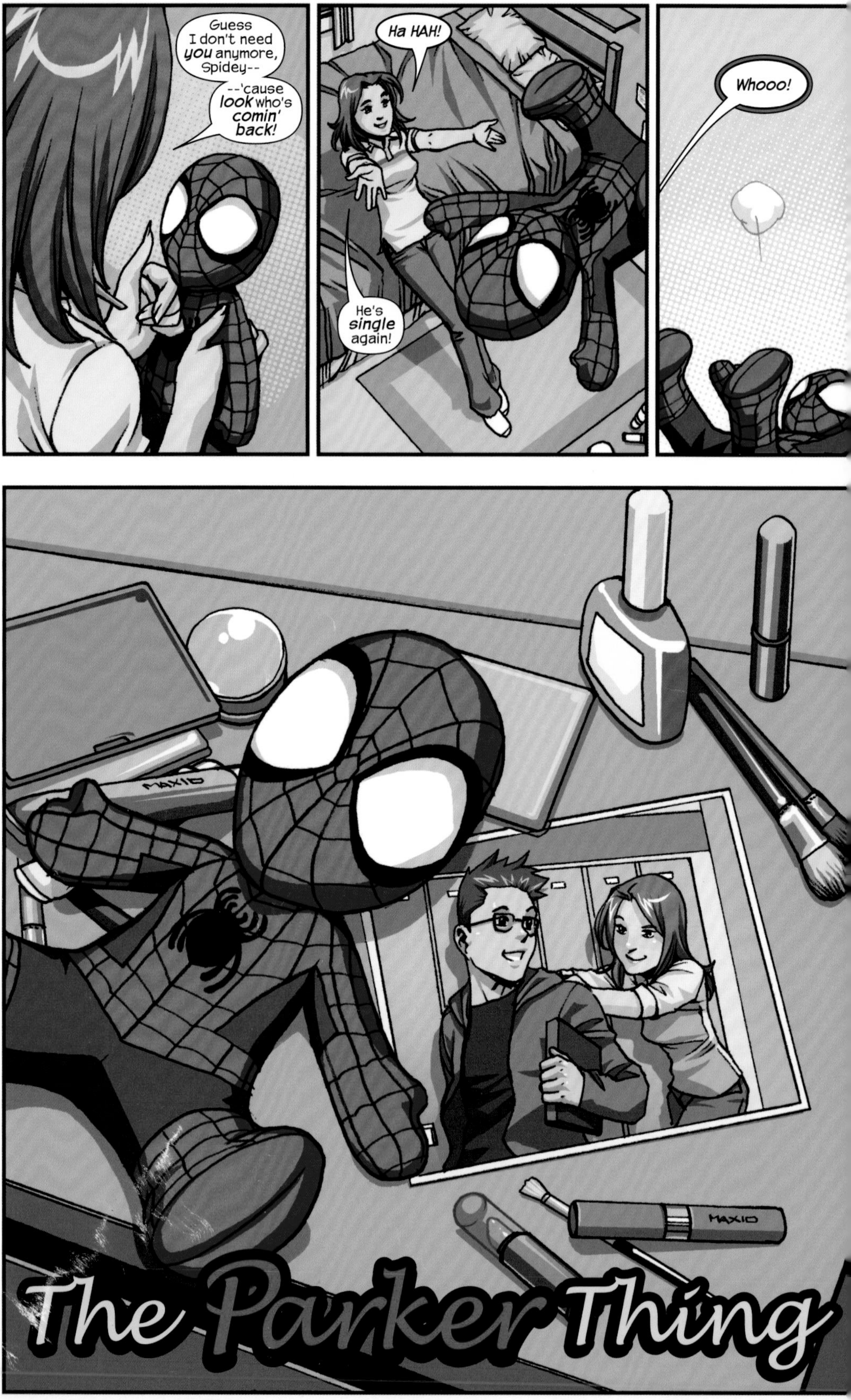
Guess I don't need *you* anymore, Spidey--
--'cause *look* who's *comin'* back!
Ha HAH!
He's *single* again!
Whooo!
MAXIO
MAXIO
The Parker Thing

MARY JANE

HARRY, FLASH & LIZ

MARY JANE

PRE-BREAK-UP   POST-BREAK-UP

Spider-Man Loves Mary Jane #6 Cover Process

BY TAKESHI MIYAZAWA

UNUSED VERSION WITH COLORS
BY CHRISTINA STRAIN

Spider-Man Loves Mary Jane #7 *Cover Process*
BY TAKESHI MIYAZAWA

Spider-Man Loves Mary Jane #9 Cover Pencils
BY TAKESHI MIYAZAWA

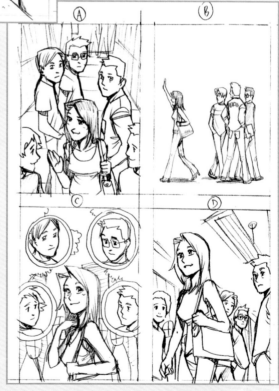

Spider-Man Loves Mary Jane # *10-11 Cover Sketches*
BY TAKESHI MIYAZAWA

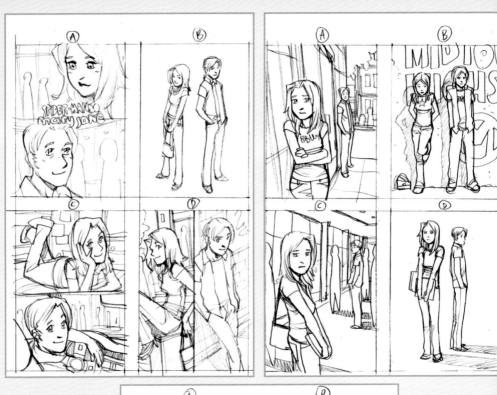

Spider-Man Loves Mary Jane **#12-13 Cover Sketches**
BY TAKESHI MIYAZAWA